FELICITY

FELICITY

Kristen Staby Rembold

Mid-List Press
Minneapolis

FIRST NOVEL SERIES

COPYRIGHT © 1994 by Kristen Staby Rembold

Published by Mid-List Press, 4324-12th Avenue South
Minneapolis, Minnesota 55407-3218

Library of Congress Cataloging-in-Publication Data
Rembold, Kristen Staby, 1957 -
Felicity / Kristen Staby Rembold.
p. cm. — (First novel series)
I. Title. II. Series.
ISBN 0-922811-19-9 (pbk.): $12.00
PS3568.E558F4 1994
813'.54—dc20   94-13615
CIP

We thank New Directions Publishing Corporation for
permission to use lines from William
Carlos Williams' poem "Widow Woman in Springtime"
© 1949 William Carlos Williams, which
appears in *Collected Poems* © 1964 New Directions.

For my family, especially my husband and daughters, my parents, and in memory of my paternal grandparents, Carl and Margaret.

The author would like to thank the Virginia Center for the Creative Arts for two fellowships which enabled her to complete this book.

1

ON THIS PARTICULAR THURSDAY EVENING, I let loose a few stray pages from the third chapter of my dissertation and watch them drift down the long chute to the incinerator. I stare for a long time down that dark rectangle, feeling its attraction. My negative energy is strong enough to engulf whole solar systems.

Later, I'm in the shower undergoing purification when the ringing telephone startles me. It's strange to be back in my own apartment after the months I spent living with Dennis.

Now my mother's voice comes urgently to me: "There's been a fire!"

I stand in the hallway, wrapped in a towel, water streaming down my legs.

"The fire began," she says, "in the upstairs kitchen."

Grandma's kitchen! I have to sit down. My towel trails across the floor, absorbing my own puddle. I close my eyes to picture the dark shape of the house, flames rising from its center.

"They had to call in the firefighters from North Garden, too," my mother is saying. "They got it contained. But the upstairs is a mess. A mess!"

"Is everyone okay?" I ask.

"Your father, your grandmother, and I are all fine, although your grandmother, poor thing, is shaken."

"And you aren't, Mom? What do you think started it?"

There is an uncomfortably long pause before Mother says calmly, "Your grandmother must have left a burner on, with something flammable nearby. The kitchen cabinets went up just like that."

I press my feet against the cool hardwood floor. Inside, I'm feeling sick. Why does my mother always refer to Grandma Katherine as my grandmother, as if the two of them were of no relation?

During the course of the week that follows, I hear in turn from each member of my family: my father, who reports that, although she may not have told me so, this mess has gotten my mother very upset; my brother, who fills in all the factual detail left out of other, more emotional reports; and, finally, near the end of the week, Grandma Katherine, who does, indeed, sound shaken and maybe even a bit confused.

I remind myself it is never good to talk with her over the phone these days; the phone no longer seems to do her justice.

The telephone barrage diverts my attention from problems, which though by no means small, assume less weight. Dennis recedes into the background, his telephone calls perceived by me as something like white noise. Perversely, I don't tell him about the fire.

I put my dissertation chapter aside for the time being and absorb myself in classwork. Still, in the back of my mind is an image of that dark house with flames rising from its center.

Then, in my graduate school mailbox, I receive a note from my mother, in her quirky, inscrutable hand. No matter what the news, my mother always sends it up in rounded letters, cheerful as balloons. But her handwriting doesn't fool me. I can sense the psychic weight of the letter as I lift it from the box. The letter reads:

> *Dear Laura,*
> *What a week we have had here. I would have called, but then I decided what I had to tell you would be easier to take if it came in writing.*
> *For some time, your father and I have been looking into other kinds of care for your grandmother, because she hasn't been doing as well, and sometimes I have to be out of the house. Now, with her living quarters destroyed, we've arranged for her to move into The Evergreens on October 1st. This news will probably upset you, but we feel it is the best possible alternative for everyone concerned.*
> *Love,*
> *Mother and Father*

If my parents had been thinking about nursing homes "for some time," why hadn't they mentioned it to me?

I let myself down on the visitor's chair. Yes, the news upsets me. But upset is too mild a word. I'm alarmed, that's what I am. A small voice somewhere inside me cries: *Oh, Grandma Katherine!*

Wendy, the departmental secretary, glances away from her computer screen and focuses on me. Pathetic as I am, I might have been on the verge of explaining, but her phone rings and I'm forgotten. Anyway, she is used to seeing distraught graduate students pace the short corridor that runs past her desk to the office of the department chair. "Distraught is how you all end up, sooner or later," I overheard her observe once, at a departmental party.

THIS VERY EVENING, I drive straight through from Chicago to the New York border. I have an image of myself, clad in splendorous virtue, determined to save my Grandma Katherine. This fantasy is quite unlike the impotence I experience in my own life, as I do not fail to notice. I feel the weight of something pressing at my back—like the dusk pressing in on me from all sides, like the dark water lapping up so close to the road on either side—in this scary wasteland south of Chicago. It is a relief to drive at night across four states, with only my headlights and instrument panel to guide me. There is no phone to jangle me with its unsettling noise. The drive provides a respite from the nightmarish downward spiral of my continuing dialogue with Dennis. It seems we are more absorbed in this ritual of parting than we ever were in being together, or even making love. It feels good to be detached, for once.

As I pass through the night, picking up on snatches of recognizable music that emerge from the fuzz of the radio, and the intermittent human voice, the sense I have of myself as loose, as unconnected, is deepened. I meet the dawn as it rises from behind the foothills of the Alleghenies and sparkles in the lake below. Somewhere in northwestern Pennsylvania, I stop to gas up, pee, and buy coffee so hot it's steaming as I drive on, sipping it and listening to the news.

The usual homecoming twinges stir me as I drive into Felicity. My aorta twitches within my abdomen like a plucked bass string. The occasional rusted pickup truck

or weathered building has all the sting of a personal
affront; they blight an otherwise fine, favorable fall
morning. The town is already playing me. I am well on
my way to an emotional day.

I have decided to ditch my car at roadside and hike the
long, steep driveway up to my parent's house. I walk with
my eyes lifted in anticipation of my first glimpse through
bronzed oak trees—first, a swatch of lemony-colored
plank siding, next the broad, gray roof. . . .

As I approach the house, I spot a lone figure sitting in
a rocker on the porch. I recall all the times I scrambled
up this hill from the school bus stop to find Grandma
Katherine sitting in that rocking chair. She would be
peeling apples or potatoes or something over a bowl, or
else reading. But she was easily distracted, and I often
came upon her when she was paused, listening, or search-
ing the sky because a bird had cried out, or the leaves of
a tree had rustled. The porch was one of her favorite
spots.

Something about Grandma is different today: her
hands contain nothing. She holds them carefully spread
across her lap, like a pair of pressed, golden leaves. She
doesn't seem alert. I drag my feet in the fallen leaves to
make a noise so that I won't startle her. "Grandma!" I
call.

"Laura!" Her face brightens with a smile of recognition. She raises herself up from the chair. Her eyes are
attentive, but she does not see me. Grandma Katherine is
blind. Nevertheless, she is headed across the porch in my
direction.

"Stay there, I'm coming!" I warn her, but she is all
purpose. Without a bit of hesitation, she steps off the edge
of the porch, having missed the two stairs, and crashes

onto the lawn. Before I can get to her, she has picked herself up with an almost athletic exuberance and is dusting off the crumbs of garden dirt.

I take her by the elbow. "Are you all right?"

"Of course!" she chortles. "How clumsy of me."

I look closely at her face, knowing she can't look back. Grandma tilts her face as though considering something far away, and the sunlight bleaches her light hair. Her face looks almost ageless; she could be young or old.

Grandma Katherine glances around expectantly, a nervous habit overriding the uselessness of her eyes. She holds her arms stiff in starched cotton sleeves; the tips of her fingers make vague contact with the chambray skirt of the dress. Katherine isn't one of those elderly ladies who feels duty-bound to wear a dress, and it is odd to see her do so, especially since it is such an inappropriate costume for moving day. Her stance is upright, and her figure sleek and firm. It takes the sight of her legs, which are discolored by alarming technicolor bruises, for me to see that she has changed.

I take in my breath and ask, "How do you feel?"

"How do you think I feel?"

At first, I have no answer, only a passing impulse to hug her, which I ignore. No matter how close we are, none of the women in my family hug each other. Or, if we do, our braced arms and unyielding shoulders constitute more of a barrier than a closeness.

I watch as a cardinal appears, then disappears in the bushes near the house. To Katherine, there is only the sound, a flickering of dry leaves. I want to take her hand and hold it up to the cardinal, if that were possible. I want to tell her how vivid the color is. I suddenly feel it is urgent news.

But I am afraid. Afraid that her reply could be: Another cardinal? *Why bother me about a common bird?*—as if another cardinal would just be excess baggage; as if after seeing perhaps a thousand, what use has she for other cardinals? I feel she is having less and less use for a lot of things. I feel she is saying goodbye.

Beyond the margin of the lawn, the meadow has turned a tawny color. The stalks of weed and grass retain a certain stiffness, a tenacity that holds them proud despite the breezes. The frosts have not yet come to bend them down, though it is only a matter of time. I remember standing in this spot as a girl, watching in awe as the turgid gray clouds of mid-November lowered the vault of the sky. It was almost as if I could glimpse Providence then, the enormity of it, and comprehend that it could swallow me.

Soon a cool wind will come scuttling close to the ground, followed by the first numbing particles of snow.

Grandma Katherine lifts her head. She can hear the pale ticking of meadow grass. I can see her slipping away from the person she once was, her spirit eroding. I swirl my tongue in my mouth and taste dust. Yes, I am old enough now. Old enough to sometimes, for an instant, sense my whole possibility dissolving into futility. But it's too painful a possibility to acknowledge.

In my darker moods, I can see the appeal of losing oneself, sinking into oblivion, but I never expected Grandma Katherine to be accepting of her own death. No, I believed death would have to come all at once, like a roof collapsing, and crush her. That vision came between the time when I unquestioningly accepted my parents' religion and the time when I took religion on as my own. It was the era of my schism.

What if the truth is more complex?

We walk side-by-side back to the house. Grandma doesn't hold her eyes closed, as some blind people do, and yet there is no animation left in them.

I wish I could know what it is Grandma knows—and isn't telling me.

The first forsaken leaves crumble beneath our feet as we come in together from the orchard. I hold her hand lightly in mine. Her skin, loose and dry as crepe paper, rasps against my open palm. The apple orchard looked much the same to me as it always has, minus a few dead limbs. Only Grandma has changed.

I say, "I don't understand why you need to go there."

Softly, she replies, "*They* need me to."

"But—" I begin, yet nothing in the sea of reasons which has been swirling inside my head seems to emerge. I know, at the heart of it, my parents are right. Still, I can't allow myself to see their decision as final. Not yet.

"It's time," she says, without conviction, as if she has memorized this explanation and has grown used to speaking in platitudes. She nods vaguely and without comprehension.

I look with some bitterness at the turning leaves this morning. It seems wrong that they should be so beautiful when she is not able to see them. I sense, for the first time, that when she dies, the world will progress in its usual way without her.

OUR HOUSE HAS ALWAYS BEEN A LOCAL LANDMARK. Although it is not the oldest structure in Felicity, it receives important mention in the Historical Society's "History of Felicity" because it served as an

Underground Railroad station during the Civil War. The house was easy to spot because it sits atop a gentle hill and, back then, it was exactly one day's travel to the Canadian border.

Another feature that distinguishes our house from others in Felicity is that my family has not always lived here. When my family moved in, in 1960, we commenced to do something revolutionary: our whole family worked together one summer to restore the house. I was only four, and so was alternately scolded and ignored, while my brother Daniel was allowed to paint the first glossy, smooth coat of white over the speckled bare woodwork.

Our renovations were tolerated by the townspeople of Felicity only because my father had grown up here. He was a local son, a college graduate, a credit to the community—even if it was strange that he moved into an old house when he could have perfectly well afforded a new one. In time, partially because fashions had changed but mainly out of respect for my father, people began to accept, even to embrace, our restoration as an improvement. Another couple decided to fix up the old inn on Main Street, and there was a drive to clean up and paint downtown Felicity that wasn't even initiated by my parents, although they later joined in.

As for me, I loved our old house from the start. It boasted numerous fireplaces and creaky floors and big windows that could even be used as doors if you lifted them up all the way. And there were plenty of secret places, like the innermost room of the cellar, which was always musty and fragrant from the bushels of apples we had stored and the bundles of herbs that hung upside-down. The central banister, oiled by our hands, was always smooth and slidable. Dozens of window seats and odd corners made it easy to go off and get lost in a book.

I am not prepared for how dark the front hall appears when I first step inside. I know it is my state of mind, but even my parents' faces look darker, slackened and hollowed by a sorrow I had never observed before.

Mother's eyes scan me in a way that seems to catalog everything. Her irises, for once, appear more gray than blue, and the stained apron she wears drains her of beauty and frivolousness. "I hope the drive wasn't too hard on you, Laura," she says.

"No," I answer, pressing my palm against her forearm in reassurance. I sweep my glance across to include my father.

"Laurie," he says, gripping me close to him and kissing me on the cheek.

I draw away from him, feeling fond but, at the same time, piercingly sad. This is the first time I have come back and found him looking older. Not that he appears haggard, but his forelock is streaked gray, the veins stand out more plainly in his hands, the skin does not seem quite so taut across his cheeks—and those things are enough.

Dad clasps me around the shoulder and inquires as to whether I am feeling any better. He says, "Your mother and I aren't worried about your grades or about that boyfriend of yours. We know those things will straighten themselves out."

What neither of them seems to want to talk about is Grandma Katherine. She follows stealthily behind me like a shadow, as if she requires my protection, and cowers in a corner of the dining room while I set the table for the family breakfast my mother has prepared.

I say nothing just then, bending over the silverware drawer so that my hair falls in to shield my face. I focus with great intensity on the selection of proper utensils. Then, with my head still lowered, I take the silverware and four of Mother's eyelet-edged blue gingham place-mats out to the dining room. When my mother grips Katherine by the shoulders and leads her to a chair as if she were an imbecile, I still remain silent, though I can't help letting my eyes bulge out a little. That indignant feeling, which had gotten me in trouble so often as a child, is welling up inside me now.

I feel mildly like a usurper, sitting in my brother Daniel's chair. He, the heir apparent, has moved out and will soon marry, now that he's graduated from architecture school. He's been made father's junior partner down at the firm. *Naturally*, I had thought after hearing the news. How could I have ever wondered what he'd decide to do? I try to keep that indignant feeling at bay, but it's difficult.

I remember once, when Mom and I were up in Katherine's living room for some reason, that Mom palmed a tiny picture in an oval frame that was sitting on one of the end tables. Frowning, she had examined it for a moment while I peered around her shoulder. The photograph, stained in that sienna range of colors, depicted a tall, confident-looking young man with his arm draped casually around a pleased blond woman who was older. Grandma Katherine, I had supposed, although excepting the shorter stature, it could have been my mother. Despite looking out across that vast expanse of time, their eyes seemed especially intense and sharp. Their blue, like the blue of the sky, translated into a burnt color. Snug in modern bathing suits, they looked brazen, incestuous maybe. I intruded enough to ask Mom, "Was that your brother who died in Korea?"

Absentmindedly, she had replied, "Ken, yes. This must have been one of his last pictures."

That made me scrutinize it all the more. "He was handsome."

"I suppose so," she sighed.

"Why weren't you in it?"

Snapping the picture shut, Mom placed it back on the table, not the way it was before. "I don't know. Maybe I was away with my friends, or even at college. They don't seem to have taken many pictures that have me in them."

I didn't say anything, because as far as I was concerned it didn't seem unusual, just a fact of life. It reminded me of our photo album, which was filled with images of my brother with his school friends at sporting events and parties. I guess, with my love of books and my fondness for just one best friend at a time, I didn't have a photogenic childhood.

Now, as I look across at Grandma Katherine, her eyes seem a darker blue than they really are, framed by the bright light pouring in from the bay window behind her. The light is enough to dim the shade of the pink begonias my mother keeps in baskets on the window ledge; enough to make the afghans draped over the matching rockers seem all filaments, like collapsed spiderwebs.

I continue watching her as she lifts a spoonful of thawed raspberries from her bowl. Illumination has turned her translucent; the substructure of her bones is barely visible beneath her skin. Her spoon wavers slightly in her hands as she lifts it toward her chin, and the juice in the spoon's deep bowl trembles. She jerks it, nowhere near her mouth. The spoon collides into her small, pointed jaw; the juice splatters on her bosom and the dark, waterlogged berries roll to her lap.

"Mother!" says my mother, standing up. She daubs her napkin in a water goblet and starts in on Katherine's dress. As she blots over and over, she scolds: "Why couldn't you have been more careful, when you knew you were wearing your only dress? Everything else is packed, you know."

"Leave her alone," I mutter. "It doesn't matter."

By the time Mom has led her off to the bathroom, Katherine looks subdued, senseless. Is it a defense? I wonder what she is thinking, whether she is thinking at all.

"Don't look at me as if I were a criminal," Mother says, but I can't help it. The napkin she holds could be blood-soaked. Not so much because of the color: it is the way that she holds it, in both hands, safely distant from her body.

"You think she doesn't need to go—but she does. She frightens even herself!"

"Laura," Dad says gently, "if only you knew about all the accidents, the falls, the fires we've had around here. I can't count the times she's lost her bearings out in the orchard and ended up wandering in the dark for hours before we found her. It simply isn't safe, not when you mother's gone so often on business. And, what's more, Katherine isn't happy here. Not with you kids gone, and no books to read, and fewer things she can help us with."

I think of her, finally blind. That disease of hers has brought more darkness by the year; it should hardly have surprised us, or her. Probably it affected her most of all the year she had to stop reading, or perhaps the year before, when she knew it was coming and knew, as well, that there were not nearly enough hours of daylight left to finish the reading she had to do for her master's degree. It was as if some overly strict parent had turned off the reading lamp, not just for one night but forever, and there was nothing like a flashlight that she could use to grapple her way through under the covers. Looking back, I can see that it must have been the beginning of death for her.

Dad goes on to explain that The Evergreens is more of a school than a nursing home. They'll teach her Braille, she'll be saved from isolation . . . but is is more than I can do to listen.

This morning, the way my family so effortlessly falls back into our old rules and patterns surprises me, though I suppose it shouldn't. After breakfast, even Katherine rouses herself, as if she were a few years younger, to help us clear the table. She starts out cautiously in the direction of the kitchen, one bony thumb hooked around her bowl. I rush up behind her, in case something should happen, but she moves soberly across the room, pausing to probe at the threshold with the blunt toe of her shoe. When she makes it over to the counter, I hear her release her breath and see a smile of relief cross her face.

Mom and Dad pause long enough from whatever they had been conferring over to look up and see her. I can tell Dad is pleased, but Mom only bites her lip and inclines her head over the stack of soiled white dishware. Dad glances over at me. "Why don't you take Katherine upstairs? I believe she wanted your help in sorting through her things."

Grandma Katherine nods, and smiles when I take her by the elbow. She clings tersely to my arm, the way I had to Dennis's the first time he had led me up to his apartment.

I think about what a different person I had been before that. Although I know I have gained many things from him, I wonder if I have lost anything in exchange. But of course I have: I've exchanged separateness and the clarity of vision that gave me for the confused intensity of involvement. And now, through circumstance, fate has offered me the chance to choose again. I try to eye the choices coolly, as if they are buffet entrees and I am about to pick out one of them using tongs. But I could never choose separateness. No, the hard, brittle, remote self I fear I could become would be too high a price to pay for personal safety.

I think what disturbs Katherine so much about her blindness is the extent to which it shuts her off from us. She doesn't want to be alone; I can see that. And possibly, just possibly, she is beginning to let down the barriers between herself and my mom. Not that Mother is. Whatever has happened to Mom, to make her so afraid of exposure?

I slide my hand sadly along the banister as we climb the last few steps. The lovely, dark wood has been painted over, and the uneven, eggshell-colored walls have been papered in calico, erasing my childhood memories. I have to sigh. That is my mother: covering things in layer after layer of material, as if to hide some essential quality she is afraid might stand out too starkly.

But never mind. We ascend a second flight of stairs up to Grandma Katherine's apartment. Here, we used to talk about the interesting bookstores she and Charles (and later I) visited in Chicago, about why not to have children if you were a woman, about World War II, about Paris and New York and London, about what college was like for her. One of the few subjects which seemed less welcome was that of my mother. As I grew to know Grandma Katherine better, I often tested her by mentioning Mom, but her reaction was nearly always the same. She would sidestep my mentions, a diversion that was never lost on me.

Just the same, it was a relief, at times, not to have to think of Mom, who dominated my life in so many of its aspects. On my way up that steep-pitched staircase, I always sensed that I was ascending to freedom. I felt free of myself, full of ideas. It was as if the air were lighter there, where we were hidden beneath, shadowed beneath the eaves of the house. Only the purest light reached us from above.

Those five years or so that Katherine spent with me as I was growing up seemed almost timeless, as if they would never end. If you had asked me then, I couldn't have guessed how many years would pass before I would experience that same feeling of release again. When it did occur, the venue had changed to Chicago, and I was spending a great deal of time alone with Dennis. We first made love on Election Night 1976; I remember that we were losing as, during the early morning hours, the television throbbed our only light. We held each other on the bed. Our stirrings turned to thrashings as the states on the map flickered over to blue, one by one, like the city lights switching off around us. It felt as if we were the only people alive.

We were the only people who mattered then, weren't we? It certainly seemed so, but then we naturally went out of our way to be alone, tramping along the edge of ice after the lake froze, eagerly leaping through the empty dunes of snow. In awe, we would watch the rookery birds that cluttered the small patch of pond thawed by constant, cold splattering of the fountain. How bright their colors appeared against the turbulent, black water. Their legs pumped frantically and they called out and displayed, as if theirs was a show meant for us alone.

When we talked, our ideas surged, like volatile chemical combinations. It was as if no one had ever experienced those same thoughts before.

Like the landscape, Dennis's apartment was a haven for us. On his sagging sofa bed, we slept so closely bound together that it was difficult to breathe, wedged in the gully we had created while, on either side of us, the soft mattress puffed up like warm, risen dough. Wrapped in woolen blankets as a buttress against the cold that leaked in through wind-exposed windows, we read textbooks together. Together, that is, until one of us would look up at the other, dispelling all concentration. Sometimes we cooked over his portable electric burner, simple dishes like noodles and cheese or rustic chili that served to satisfy our hunger. For, inexplicably, we often were hungry at odd hours of the day and night, hungry in the sharp obtrusive sense I imagine pregnant women are. Never have I been so hungry since. In fact, I've let go of hunger altogether. In recent months, I've become finicky in respect to many things. If someone tried to press my life into my mouth using a spoon, I suspect I'd jerk my face away, reject it.

And what has all this got to do with Katherine? It's a state of mind: the same force that held me motionless through entire novels up in Katherine's apartment also fueled the good, harsh poetry I had written on Dennis's formica-topped desk as I looked out the window at a seething, wintry Lake Michigan. I remember how the waves would suddenly shudder free of ice and beat insistently against the breakwalls, the sidewalks even. But I need to know why, since then, I haven't found it possible to write anything of value.

There is another thing, too. I have the same feeling this morning, when I first step through Katherine's door, that I had the time I turned back to view Dennis's apartment just before I left him. I have to keep reminding myself that her room isn't really dead, it just feels that way—with the smoke-scorched walls, the broken windows, the heaps of rubbish, and scattered books. And we hold onto each other and cry, Grandma Katherine and I, just like Dennis had cried when he saw me with my loaded duffel.

2

WHEN GRANDMA KATHERINE first came to live with us, the December after Grandpa Schrier died, her pale face had appeared in the darkness just beyond the safe halo of the porch light. Snow flurries flew about her head. The night seemed dark in contrast. It was bitter blue cold that night. The blast of air she let in was enough to chill the house for hours. She was, or so it seemed, a specter—as if she had died instead of my grandfather. Which, no doubt, she had in a sense. But, in other ways, I had been wrong about her.

Death was the last thing Grandma Katherine had wanted then, despite my initial impression. When she had fled from death, her escape had brought her to Felicity. Her face was only pale from the shock of the encounter. She confessed to me that first night, up in my room: "I can't go back there. Everyone there is dying!"

Or maybe there was more ambivalence in her than I care to remember. After all, she had very nearly died herself, a month later, from influenza. And how could I forget those last lines of that Williams poem she made me recite to her while she was lying so still in bed: *I feel I would like / to go there / and fall into those flowers / and sink into the marsh near them.* Those words still singe me, as though I had been branded with them.

The last time I had spoken to Grandpa, he told me he didn't want me to see him in the hospital. I protested: "I've been to hospitals before. I'm not worried about what I'll see."

I had to keep my voice down because my parents were in the next room, looking over the evening paper. I was so angry with him that I withheld a piece of news I knew he would have enjoyed: my selection as editor for the school paper.

"You're just as stubborn as I am!" he shouted into the telephone, and I could picture him raised up on one elbow before he hung up.

"TELL ME ABOUT GRANDPA," I used to ask my mother when I was little.

If Mom was in an expansive sort of mood, she would recite a story about him as she peeled carrots or punched out cookies. "I remember," she told me once, "how he'd take me into his office and find me my own desk and my own supply of drawing paper."

And Mom told me about baseball games at Wrigley Field, and about father-daughter fishing excursions into Minnesota and farther north, into Canada. She once showed me a snapshot taken in Minnesota, near a fringe of woods, in which he was a rigidly handsome German man and she, his smiling towheaded daughter.

Still, my mother's repertoire of stories was limited, and no doubt she portrayed her father as the man she wished he would be, rather than as the man he mostly was. I had no proof, really, except for my own impression of him, and Mom's allusions to his strictness, but I pictured him as a forbidding kind of father, a father from whom it would be difficult to elicit approval.

As I grew older, I became aware that Grandpa's attention seemed to demand something of me. Just what, I wasn't sure at first, but I began to realize that it was my quickness to respond to his questions, my willingness to debate that gave him satisfaction. His coldly serious face would warm from blue to slightly crimson in tone; that would be the signal that I'd pleased him. So intent was I in pursuing this reaction, so drawn by the fierce magnetism of his blue-black eyes, that the rest of my family seemed to me dim in comparison.

Once Grandpa died, I felt the need to know something about him more strongly. Who was this man who had sent me books and asked for book reports, this man who owned a desk that no one dared touch, and yet who secretly procured candies from its top right-hand drawer and slipped them into the hands of little girls? What force in him demanded the painstaking ledgers he kept of family accounts and the daybreak calisthenics? It wasn't until later that I would turn to Grandma Katherine for the answers.

IT WAS DECEMBER, 1968. I was twelve. I played Saint-Saens on my cello for the state music competition, and I learned poetry in Tom Manchester's English class.

Tom Manchester played Simon and Garfunkel records, and he smiled like a pirate with his one silver front tooth. He was a bantam-weight man, no taller than I was even at the age of twelve, but he was a stalwart member of the Catholic Church and father to a new child each year—twelve so far, with the oldest a year ahead of me in school, the youngest still a babe-in-arms. I liked his children—who were dark-haired and dark-eyed, quiet and witty as foxes—almost as much as I liked the man himself. He encouraged the class to write poetry of any kind, even street poetry, once he switched off the phonograph and there was only the deluge of snow outside to distract us. I remember my ideas coming phrase by phrase, halting at first and then flowing, as I watched the ever-changing patterns of white against the dark field of evergreen.

I wasn't usually aware of time passing as I wrote. The only awareness I kept was of Tom Manchester striding down the aisles. He was so energetic, it was difficult to contain him within the confines of a classroom. He might have happily made his living outdoors in the construction trades—I could picture him in navy blue watch cap and plaid shirt. I wrote on, unselfconsciously, knowing that at some point he would pause beside my desk to read over my shoulder. I'd hear him chuckle appreciatively at my attempts at satire. Or he'd lift my paper, ask if I'd mind if he read it aloud. Once or twice, when I couldn't help but put down heartfelt or grieving verse, he put a hand on my shoulder, and I knew he'd understood.

Tom Manchester asked me to come and work for him on Saturday mornings, teaching swimming for Town Rec. The new indoor pool had just opened, and the Saturday afternoon free swim was immensely popular with the citizens of Felicity, who considered the pool, with its tropic air, its vibrant banks of florescent lights, to be just this side of decadent. These were people used to unbroken months of dull weather, which they spent in heavy clothing, lacking for fresh air and for light. Like them, I was made heady by the touch of warm air against my bare skin, and did not question my luck at having the privilege to dive into an empty pool to do my laps before the children came. I spent the morning manipulating children's legs into a frog kick. I played dunking games with circles of toddlers. The backs of floating children's heads rested on my palm, while I explained that all it took was faith, that they had to let go and believe the water would hold them up.

The weather during that December had been unusual—thaw and freeze and then thaw and freeze again. Many days, I watched flurries race against the dark field of trees. But mostly the snow melted before it could accumulate much. Finally, just before school let out for vacation, a good snow came—twelve inches the first day, more than two feet eventually—and it stayed.

On a Saturday early in January when lessons at Town Rec had been cancelled, Tom Manchester had decided to go ice skating alone on a pond near where he lived, outside of town. On Monday, the school principal made the announcement: Tom Manchester had fallen through the ice and drowned.

I was, like everybody else, aghast, speechless. How could anyone that vital be here one moment, gone the next? But also, I tried to imagine how it must have been for him before the accident, in quiet save for the wind, isolated by empty fields of snow, with only the glide of his skates beneath him—in short, pure poetry.

Town Rec cancelled the rest of the swimming lessons after Tom died, and I took up skiing. I had to wake up early and alone each Saturday. I dressed quickly in the heavy thermal layers I wore to ski.

I remember it was a relief to hear Dad's heavy footfall on the stairs. He shrugged a coat on over his pajamas and we made our way out across the yard, breaking through the crystalline crust of snow that I wished we could have left undisturbed. As we coasted down Hill Street, between the static rows of trees, the engine thrumped. By the time it had warmed, we were already on Main Street, moving smoothly past Sandy's Dry Goods and Robertson's Hardware & Appliance and the abandoned Mobil station with its rusting Pegasus and unplowed drifts of snow. I was thinking about how none of the kids would want to talk about Tom Manchester or my grandpa dying, and how I was glad they wouldn't. Most of all, I wanted things to be normal.

Inside the bus filled with other skiiers, muffled conversations went on around me. The atmosphere was still one of sleep, the air tinged with the faint scents of milk, of breakfast eggs, of bacon smoke. Occasionally, I could hear the snag of a yawn, or make out sentence fragments. As I stared out the window past my seat-mate Joanne, I was stricken by the purity of the narrow pavement as it contrasted with the empty fields of snow. At the crest of the first ridge, we encountered the ruin of a barn. We followed the road down into a small town and then, to our left, there rose another row of green-gray hills. It is the habit of the terrain here, at this far northwestern terminus of the Allegheny Mountains: ridge, then valley, ridge, then valley, each progressively higher than the last. The character of these hills and valleys changes according to the time of year, so that in the spring the ridges are tinted blue; in the winter, gray; red-orange in the fall; and sometimes, at the end of long, summer days, the green hills appear almost purplish in tone.

Mostly these valleys are farming-places, just like my own town, only more remote. Where the snow had blown away, the fields showed corn stubble. Woodpiles shouldered up against the sides of houses. Turning onto Omphalius, the bus labored straight up the steep face of a hill. A change in the style of houses, to chalets, marked our passage. We were in ski country.

Joanne nudged me. "Earth to Laura!"

Funny she should have said that, because the place where we were then, with its ever-present swirling clouds of snow, was close to the visual image I had of heaven. Not that I had a clear formulation, or knew, for sure, what I believed. Sometimes at night I cast out my fortune. I went through the whole process: laying out the cards, reading signs from the pictures. I don't know why it should have been comforting, but it was. Everything right then seemed possible, and yet I had no sure way of knowing what was going to happen to me.

"Don't look now," said Joanne, brushing back a handful of her luxuriant auburn hair, "but Victor Garlick has been staring at you all this time."

Not many boys expressed an interest in me, compared with the number who sought out Joanne, so I was, naturally, mistrustful. I peeled off that week's ski tag and attached it to my jacket. "What makes you so sure he wasn't looking at you?" I whispered back.

I stole a look in Victor's direction. What made him so shameless that, when I caught him looking, he did not glance away? Although I had always known Victor—he was a friend of my brother's—I found myself assessing him more positively. He was four grades ahead of me, a high school sophomore, and at least an inch or two taller. Beneath my turtleneck, I could feel the blond hair on my forearms prick up, against the grain. I rubbed both arms briskly. What was it about me that he found so interesting?

Late that past summer or early that fall, Joanne and I had stolen off to one of the more remote horse pastures behind her house with the brand-new Polaroid she had just gotten for her twelfth birthday. We stripped naked and, standing knee-high in orchard grass, shot pictures of each other. Why, I don't remember now, but I think it was the result of one of her dares. How embarrassed I had felt, posing with my arms clasped behind my head as she had directed, while at the far end of the field the horses stood watching instead of grazing. Joanne solemnly carried the exposed pieces of film, wet and fragile as new butterfly wings, to a nearby rock where she counted over them and rubbed them with a chemical wand. When my figure materialized out of darkness, we both gasped. How ripe I looked, with my fledgling breasts so taut, and my long legs, and my hips and tummy still as formless as a little girl's. I, who had never considered myself anything but ugly, was lost in admiration until Joanne whistled and said, "Sex-y! Wait 'til the boys find out, they won't be able to keep their hands off!"

Then she snatched that picture out of my hand and quickly gathered up the others. She ripped the pictures of herself neatly in quarters, and teased that she would distribute mine in school.

Of course, to my knowledge, she never did. But I felt as though, by acting foolishly, I had betrayed the adults who believed in me. Joanne scrutinized my face, but I refused to give her the satisfaction of knowing my thoughts.

When the bus came to a stop outside the resort, I was the first to disembark. With my skis slung over one shoulder, I climbed the steps up to the lift area with deliberate speed. I couldn't deal with Joanne's teasing. Would I always feel so strange and serious?

My eyes were tearing up. I squinted, hard, at the horizon, so I wouldn't cry. I pictured myself alone among the thin trees near the summit. There would be a slight breeze. The only sound would be the sound of my skis.

I watched hopefully as, pair by pair, the skiers were lofted skyward. I wondered whether, if I spent enough time alone, if I could get myself to concentrate, I would hear again from Grandpa or Tom Manchester. I knew I couldn't see them or touch them again. I wanted to know they would still be there at the important times, that they would find a means to signal the approval I so badly needed.

Victor arrived, panting, beside me in line just two chairs before I would have gone up by myself. He grinned arrogantly. "Mind if we share this ride?"

I slipped my hands out of the pole straps. "No, I guess not." Then we scrambled up to the line and waited, crouched, for the chair to swing around behind us.

We were scooped up and carried a wobbly fifty feet or so beyond the building before the chair came jerking to a stop. We swung easily, back and forth, in free air. Victor laughed and kicked his skis, accentuating the motion. His laugh was surprisingly high and skittish, like it was out of his control. "You must be bad luck. I think we're only going to get one run in before lessons," Victor said.

I resisted my urge to pull down on the safety bar. I asked Victor how he liked high school, because I read somewhere that people like it when you ask them to talk about themselves.

"The sports are great." He grinned. "I was in J.V. football and basketball, and now I'm anxious for baseball to start up. If you're going into high school next year, you ought to look into being a cheerleader."

"No, thanks," I said, but I smiled at the compliment. "I'd rather stay in orchestra and work on the school paper. I work on the middle school paper now," I said, then recalled that we no longer had our advisor. "I did a lot of work on the issue that memorialized Mr. Manchester. I wonder what we'll do without him."

"They'll find you another advisor," Victor said.

"It won't be the same."

Victor threw the wadded backing from his ski pass down onto the slope.

"Don't you care about the environment?" I protested.

Victor smiled, sheepishly. "Sure, but here they'll pick up after you."

A blast of wind-driven ice crystals compelled me to pull my scarf up over my face. I focused on the skiers moving past below; their bright clothing made them seem remote. I envied them their movement; on the chair lift, I was a prisoner of the cold.

Suddenly, the lift rumbled and started up again. Victor leaned forward and studied my face. He asked, "Are you feeling cold, or something?"

"Yes, a little," I said.

Victor glanced behind, then leaned closer to me. "I could help you to get warmer." He slipped his arm around my shoulder.

I could hardly feel his hand through all my clothing, but still I leaned into his embrace.

"There, does that feel better?" he asked, and I nodded. Then, very tenderly, with his other hand, he loosened my scarf and kissed me lightly on the mouth.

My skis thudded against ground. Fortunately, I recovered my balance before the lift reached the top of the hill. Victor skied away from me and waited. I thrust my hands back into the pole straps, and stomped several times to check my bindings. Out of the corner of my eye, I saw some of Victor's friends dismount two and three chairs behind us. They swooped down toward Victor, almost knocking him over.

"Hey, did we just catch you two mixing Chapstick?" Kevin said. He raised his heavy eyebrows and directed his wide smirk in my direction. I knew Kevin would make sure my brother heard of this.

Victor's face reddened; he cast me a helpless look.

I turned my back and headed down the chute toward Avalanche, hoping to impress Victor and his friends. No one else was skiing my way, but I didn't mind so much. Giant pines closed in to narrow the path before me; voices from adjoining slopes faded away. My tracks were the only ones to mar the fresh snow. They undulated behind me, like thread from a rolling spool. Then, abruptly, the trees allowed an opening on the right, and the path ahead went no farther.

Beyond the turn, the slope was steep in its pitch and untouched in its whiteness, only about ten feet wide. Despite the gray sky, it glittered like a shimmery white runner rolled down between the stands of viridian trees. The silence was complete. I felt anxious, but I attempted a few turns, followed by steep traverses. I could not shake the feeling that I was out of control. Bracing myself against my poles, I set off again, but at too sharp an angle, so that I was aimed straight down the hill. The trees whipped by me too quickly on either side; I envisioned myself flying through the large picture windows of the restaurant at the bottom. I tumbled over several times, but the snow was deep and soft. It seemed warmer than the air.

When I tried, I could not stand up. My right leg and ski were twisted behind me. Lifting my head, I glanced around and was struck by a frigid breeze. My leg was beginning to throb. I kept thinking back to the kiss, although I'd been kissed before and knew it probably didn't mean anything. I was tangled in the skis, so I released them, and watched as they picked up speed, gliding down the hill parallel to each other. I realized that I couldn't imagine where I was going, either, and there was no way that anyone could tell me.

3

I'M LOOKING OUT FROM GRANDMA'S WINDOW, breathing deeply of the fresh air. Back inside, the atmosphere is oppressive—and not just from smoke.

It's as if the weight of all my relationships rests on their endings, but I need to remember their beginnings, too. More than a decade ago, with Grandpa and Tom Manchester dead, and Victor's first kiss still replaying itself in my mind, I remember leaning out my window in the moony way adolescents have, looking out on the same landscape I see today, when a movement caught my eye. Grandma Katherine was hurtling across the backyard with her arms spread outward to catch the wind. She's flying, I thought. Her speck-small, silhouetted form moved across the light spring horizon like a molecule unleashed. Then she turned and careened recklessly through the old orchard trees, her fingertips brushing the sprouts of new leaves. Never since have I seen Grandma Katherine with that same look of abandon and happiness all at once.

That is when our friendship began. It was the the first time she impressed me positively enough to bring out my admiration. In a similar way, I was attracted to my cheeky girlhood friend, Joanne, after seeing her fearlessly gallop her pony across a rocky pasture. As for Dennis, something in me surged for him when, late one fall, I spotted him swimming in frigid Lake Michigan. He was visible only as a wave is, as an interruption from the gray of the water. He did not thrash, but rather stroked, calmly lapping the length between breakwalls.

In the weeks before my chance observation of Grandma Katherine, I had begun to notice the slightest increase her known activities: that is, the muffled rustlings and movements I could hear from down below, in my room. It was as if a giant nymph had swelled within the tired cocoon of our attic and was just then beginning to urge off its innermost wrappings, to unfold its moist wings and beat them against the plaster walls.

I could hear Grandma Katherine's footsteps move above me when I was shut up in my room. Sometimes I'd be sitting with my legs up on the shiny green satin love seat, thinking I was reading, when all of a sudden I'd notice I was really spending time listening to her. The first time I realized that, I think I was reading the part in *The Diary of a Young Girl* when Anne Frank listens to the Van Daans. The sounds made by Grandma Katherine became more interesting and frightening as weeks passed: falling objects so heavy they made the whole house shudder with reverberations; collapsed stacks of things that spilled across the floor like mammoth dominoes; bricklike objects that slammed against walls. Sooner or later, it occurred to me that she was unpacking, sorting through, and shelving books. During my quieter moments, which I invariably spent with my feet hung over the love seat while engrossed in the writings of Austen or one of the Brontës, I would imagine Grandma Katherine reading, too. In the stillness of my own reflection, I could almost envision her crabbed hands gripping the leather binding, could almost detect the faint whisper of a leaf turning over . . .

And there were other times during the late spring of her first year with us that I began to sense a connection between us. Although there were many such nights, I remember one night in particular when I was banished to my room, a punishment that seemed arbitrary and undeserved after a dinner table argument I thought I'd won. I flipped on the radio and stirred around inside my room, moved by the music's erratic wails of protest, the constant drubbing of background drums. I sang along and lit a cigarette.

Not until the sound of my own voice died did I hear the knocking at my door. The sound made me start, though it was not angry or abusive, but sharp and businesslike: a summons.

"Who's there?" I inquired, trying as best I could not to sound startled. I tossed the lighted butt out the window and watched it sail down, close to the side of the house. It landed just below my window in a bed of green-gray ivy. After a moment, it still was smoldering, and I could detect—or perhaps just imagined—the faint bitterness of burning; I pictured the dry leaves curling, maimed by heat.

I turned down the music in time to hear a small, pointed voice reply: "It's Katherine."

"Grandma! I thought everyone else was gone." It suddenly struck me that she must know everything that had been going on inside my room.

"Everyone else is," she answered, from the other side of the door. "That leaves me and you, and I stopped by to see if you'd be interested in a game of gin, or canasta. Anything. It's so darn quiet out here!"

I felt Grandpa's spirit move in to fill the moment's
space. I sensed, though I could not see, Katherine's shoulders quiver. "Really?" I asked. "You think it will be all
right?" Cautiously, I opened the door a crack and peered
out.

Strangely, in the absence of light, Grandma Katherine
appeared particularly slight, as if the edges of her form
had bled off into darkness. Her facial features seemed
sharper. She rotated her head slowly, sniffing the air, but
said nothing.

"I suppose, if no one's here, it wouldn't matter," I said,
and allowed myself to slip over the threshold. I flicked on
the hall light, dispelling shadows. "What happened, anyway?"

Katherine motioned me up the stairs. "Not a thing.
Daniel decided to go over to the Schultzes' with them.
Your mother was being oversensitive, you know."

I nodded and blinked because I could feel the water
floating in my eyes. I was perplexed by the power of my
feelings. And I wished Mother did not affect me so much.

"They've been gone for over an hour. I have to say, I
was happy to hear you put the music on." Katherine
reached up and flipped a switch that flooded the room
with light.

Her room was vast and dreamy, unlike any other room
in our old house. From near the apex of the roof, sky-
lights peered up into the heavens. Although I did not say
so, I was disappointed that I could not see stars.

"I liked that song," Grandma Katherine said defini-
tively. "Surprisingly, at my age, I sometimes feel that way,
too."

"Grandma, you don't look all that old to me," I protested. "Sometimes you seem closer to my own age than Mom does."

"That's the sad part. I still feel the same things; it's just that I'm trapped in this rickety, old body. I thought, when I got to be this age, it would seem right, but it doesn't. I want to say, 'It couldn't be time yet! It's all passed too quickly!'"

Katherine sighed. Her fine-boned hands gently tugged at the woolen elbows of her cardigan. "Now, what do you say we get started in on those cards?"

After a moment's digging, she had located the cards in the pencil drawer of a writing desk, and tossed them from there to the coffee table.

"Mind sitting on the rug?" she called over her shoulder as she disappeared into her tiny kitchen and returned with a tray of refreshments.

She sat cross-legged on the rug with me. Snapping the rubber band from the cards onto her wrist, she shuffled back and forth expertly. "Cocoa and crackers," she said, nodding toward the tray. "I know you didn't have enough to eat."

Shyly, I helped myself. Had she asked me if I were hungry, I would have said I wasn't. I was, but the physical differences between us made me self-conscious. It wasn't that I was awful-looking—I looked okay to myself—but my figure was nothing like the slender build I wished I had. Not like tiny Katherine, or my tall, model-svelte mother, who would never have offered me a bedtime snack. At mealtimes, Mother exercised her not inconsiderable gift for derision. So, gratefully, I sipped from the cocoa and fanned out my hand to examine the cards.

Grandma Katherine looked me straight in the eye, searchingly, and after seeming to contemplate whether or not to make some further inquiry of me, she thought better of it, and we got down to the business of playing cards.

I glanced around the room, trying to take in as much as I possibly could. I observed that my architect father had incorporated a wall of built-in bookshelves into his design and that Katherine had filled them with a marvelous collection of volumes. I knew this already, but to actually look upon them was splendid. I was able to spot Pearl S. Buck, Hawthorne, Hemingway, and Steinbeck, but I was as yet unfamiliar with most of the authors. Dostoevsky? Zola? Such names were too much for a twelve year old.

Scanning her collection reminded me of the books Katherine and my grandfather Charles used to send me each birthday and Christmas: books that were not really meant for children, like *David Copperfield* and *The Scarlet Pimpernel* and *Pride and Prejudice*, with tooled-leather covers and fancy endpapers and illustration plates separated from the other pages by sheets of tissue paper. I prized these books and enshrined them on the top shelf of my bookcase. Katherine's books were every bit as fine.

Grandma Katherine, glancing up from her cards, caught me lost in admiration. "I know you're fond of books," she told me, "so keep in mind that you're welcome to borrow mine."

"Does reading about things ever make you feel sad?" I asked. "I mean, like having some kind of idea that you can't use, or becoming interested in something when there are no books about it, and no one to teach you?"

"Yes," Grandma Katherine said thoughtfully, almost inwardly, as if to thwart my sudden attention.

I, too, was embarrassed by my own intensity, and by hers—by the exposure we had created there, in that room so white and stripped of curtains, where there was no place to hide.

Grandma Katherine creased her paper napkin over and over with her thumbnail. She was not looking at me. "Would it make any sense to you if I told you that, although I miss Charles very much, now I realize that being with him kept me from things I could have done firsthand? Maybe I could have been an English professor, myself."

I didn't answer.

She pulled her lips into a slight grimace, and veiled her expression, as nimbly as if she were snapping down a window blind.

I REMEMBER ONE DAY, while Grandma Katherine and I were out picking apples together—she was at the basket, I was in the tree—I ventured to ask her about Grandpa.

She held a perfect Winesap in her hand; her face warmed to a smile. "Well, I met him in one of my first literature classes. I was fresh off the farm, and it must have been his first year as a professor. I found it strange that, here in America, I should have an English professor whose accent was stronger than mine."

I leaned forward, against the knobby substance of the branch, and tried to imagine Grandma Katherine as a young farm girl, with long blond braids and clear blue eyes. My hand brushed the silvery green apple leaves. Love stories were my favorite kind.

"The accent wasn't exactly the same—my people were Low German, his were High—but it was familiar enough to make me homesick. It made me think back to my father, who was struggling so hard to send all his seven children to college, and to my mother, who did back-breaking work and had little education. I was glad to be gone, and yet I had a secret feeling of warmth for him, because he reminded me of home."

"What made him notice you?" I asked.

I could just barely see her below me in the dappled light. She was looking down thoughtfully; her hand brushed over the top of the apples. "It was so long ago, but I think it had to do with the fact that I saw him for what he was. And that's the way he saw me, too. He was brilliant, even then, and I was a bright girl, a clever student. We admired each other.

"Then one day, after our final class, I was unwrapping a piece of plum kuchen when he came up behind me. He asked me if I wouldn't break off a little piece for him. It was something his mother used to make and he was homesick for, he said, just like he was homesick for girls like me. Well, there he was, looking taller than he had ever looked on stage, and I said, 'of course,' but my hand was shaking as I broke my piece of kuchen in two. We were standing under elm trees, and I remember how oddly he looked at me. I didn't understand why until I offered him the cake. Once he had touched me, he wouldn't let go of my hand. We stood for a long time like that, with the sun coming down on us in patches, as if it had been meant to be that way."

That was the beginning of what she told me about Grandpa over the years. Once they were married, things changed. "I should have been suspicious," Grandma

Katherine said, "the way he kept urging me to drop out of school. But how would I have known any better at that age, and with my upbringing? I completed my degree, but everyone complained about the waste of time, of money, of effort. Even my father felt marrying my professor was good enough for me."

For the first two years they were married, she worked as a librarian. Despite her job, no minor point of housekeeping could be overlooked: that was a part of their contract she understood. "It pleased me," she recalled, "to be strong that way. He was so proud and so handsome, and I was so much in love. It was relatively simple to see to his needs, and when I did, it made both of us happy."

In due time, Charles decided that he wanted a child. Katherine, although this was one of the things she knew was expected of her, was secretly terrified. She sensed that Charles would no longer permit her the library job which he had merely tolerated before. "Maybe that's why I hid it from him, after I knew. No matter how often I would have to leave the kitchen while I was making supper, and closet myself in the bathroom to retch, I always came out smiling."

He was furious, of course, when he finally did find out, and he made quick arrangements for Katherine's dismissal from the library. Afterward, he seemed satisfied, blissful even, and Katherine did her best to reconcile herself to the change. "It will be better this way," he pronounced, and that was how Mother was born, into a hastily settled domesticity.

AS A YOUNG CHILD, I had felt a bit overlooked by Grandma Katherine. I sensed Mother had been too, because during our visits to her parents' house in Chicago, she had spent excessive amounts of time with me, seizing me from the company of others abruptly, without warning, and taking me on abbreviated walks around that elegant block of brass-trimmed townhouses. I remember how briskly Mother walked, so that she was practically dragging me, and how she sometimes rushed out of the house in such a hurry that she forgot to take our jackets.

My grandparents' indifference toward me passed with time. When my mother still insisted on storming out of the house on occasion, she at least had a companion in my brother. Actually, I felt strangely pleased to stay behind, although I was less than enthralled with the stuffy atmosphere in my grandparents' living room and the tiresome dialogues that went on between my grandfather and my father. In those days, while Grandpa Schrier was still alive, Grandma Katherine kept silent during these conversations, despite the obvious interest she displayed with her sharp nods and occasional murmured disapprovals. Whenever Grandma Katherine became more serious, she leaned a little forward, and waves of her silver-tipped blond hair fell in and curled around her cheekbones and mixed with her faint white brows. She stirred the air with her bony hands and energy seemed almost to radiate from her pale fingertips. The only person she had dared to be outspoken with, then, was my mother.

It wasn't until Grandpa had died, and Grandma Katherine had come to live with us, that I discovered how resentful my mother felt about being overlooked by her parents. She and Katherine didn't fight the way she and I did—gathering clouds followed by a pure bolt stroke of hostility, then silence. They didn't actually fight at all. But something had been wedged in between them, something too large and too ingrown to be forced out easily. It sometimes seemed their words, their actions, were choreographed to avoid that hard place between them. They dwelled on a limited number of conversational topics— cooking, PBS television, gardening, and bestsellers—like overly solicitous acquaintances. Whenever they did happen to stumble headfirst into each other, their sharp words didn't come close enough to the spot to mitigate its poison. I used to imagine—and I feared the possibility— that some day the spate of real words would come, and it would splatter down like the corrosive rain of nearby steel towns.

Watching the two women feel out the perimeters of their barrier, I felt nothing but dismay. My loyalty was compromised by my respect for both of them. I tried as best I could not to allow their remarks to provoke me from my uninvolvement. Just the same, my objectivity failed me from time to time. Sometimes it happened willingly, sometimes without my notice.

Naturally, I had felt curious about Grandma Katherine. Intrigued by her. And when she invited me up to use her books, I let go of my inherent reticence which formerly had kept me away. It never occurred to me that Grandma Katherine's favoritism toward me, and my choice to spend time with her, could possibly have hurt my mother.

Once, when I was standing just outside our kitchen door with a bucket of freshly shelled peas, something, some detectable charge in the atmosphere, held me there at the threshold. Held me, watching. Though I could hardly make out the shapes of their wiry, bare arms as they hauled pots from stove to sink through the thick, clotted steam, I could feel the tension between Mom and Grandma Katherine. I sensed it had to do with me. But why? What had I done? I pressed my forehead against the slippery, hard framework of the door.

Then it came to me: I had mentioned my excitement about a summer college program for high school students. My enthusiasm vanished when I saw my mother's jaw tighten. Her voice turned arch in reply. "Have you forgotten, young lady, that in order to go to college, you have to work over the summers?"

Standing at the door with the bucket handle pressing into my palm, I could see the tension between Mom and Grandma Katherine had everything to do with me. So, full of wonder, and pricked by a sliver of dread, I observed the women as they moved numbly, like sleep-walkers, through the turbid vapor. Beyond the clanging pans and the rush of water, I could hear the muffled sound of their voices.

As they eased a heavy stream of peas and hot water out over a colander, I heard Grandma Katherine's voice. "You know, Kate, Laura's capable of so much more than you allow, or encourage her to do."

"I don't know what you mean, Mother," Mom said stiffly. I couldn't see her—by then, I had retreated and was standing in a corner just adjacent to the open door—but her face would have betrayed no emotion.

"I'm not trying to butt in," Katherine insisted, "but it does seem as though Daniel gets more in the way of opportunities around this house."

"If that's not butting in, then what is it?" my mother said in her quiet, furious voice as she scrubbed her hands fiercely beneath icy water. "I didn't meet your expectations, so now you're trying to take Laura away from me, and make her into the daughter you wished for."

I was so moved by my mother's words that I emerged from my hiding place. I must have stirred something in the silence between them. They both turned to look at me. Grandma Katherine's eyes were soft, full of feeling, but Mother's were hard and vacant of expression. I should have told my mother that no matter how much Grandma Katherine loved me, she was the one I wanted. I tried to tell her with my faint smile as I handed her the bucket of peas. But whatever hardness there was in her failed to dissolve, and oftentimes since, I have looked up and seen it glittering in her eyes.

4

THOUGH WE HAD GROWN UP SIDE-BY-SIDE, my brother
Daniel and I were to each other remote foreigners. In contrast to Daniel's, my world was limited to the confines of
home, school, and books. While he worried about sol-
diery, I read *Nicholas & Alexandra* and wondered about
the fate of Madame Nhu. He left the house for sporting
events, parties, and dates, returning from each of these
with a different, but distinct foul smell. His manner var-
ied, it seemed to me, only between braggadocio and
secrecy. He was thinking about college, war, sports, and
sex. I concentrated instead on the rule of our own small
kingdom and worried about our collective fate.

Back in the 1960s, the Felicity civil defense sirens
would take up their scary wail every Tuesday afternoon.
No matter where we were or what we were doing, we were
expected to stop, drop, and cover. Even as a child, I
thought the drill made little sense. I remember the
teacher leading the class out of the classroom into the
corridor lined with beige metal lockers that reverberated
with the ugly blast of the alarm. We walked in a straight
line with our hands over our ears and bugged-out eyes,
like children of the Holocaust, to our lockers where we
were expected to squat and cover our heads, waiting for
the bomb that never came. I peered up sometimes, doubting

that my arms would protect me from such a thing as an atom bomb, but my elders knew better, and an adult hand always materialized to shove my head back down. I have to give the teachers credit for maintaining an air of urgency; none of us was ever completely sure whether it was a drill or whether, through some political development we had missed or couldn't understand, war had been declared.

My father was a friend of the town's civil defense director, Bill Russell, a tall, athletically-built man who wouldn't have looked out of place with a whistle around his neck, though in fact he was mild-mannered in spite of his looks. My father and he are still friends. Mr. Russell lives in the same place, down across from the post office in the house with the forest green trim, although many things have happened to him. His daughter Kimberly, who was always too beautiful for her own good, fled Felicity for a modeling job in New York City, where it turned out she was in over her head. She got mixed up with some seamier sorts and eventually was murdered.

But back in the 1960s, Mr. Russell conspired, along with the other town fathers, to keep the citizens of Felicity safe, beyond the reach of outside forces. What thoughts raced through the minds of those young family men as they posted the yellow-and-black shelter signs at strategic locations and arranged for the storage of canned food in basement cupboards? What did they discuss at their meetings? Who among them had decided to take action, and for what reasons?

Did the world seem as though it were about to end back then? I've always wondered. The adults around me gave no clue, although they did tend to linger over the evening news, and I was sometimes shushed or shooed out of the television's way so they could watch without interruption. Nothing remarkable happened in Felicity during those years.

Later, during the Vietnam War, some of my junior high classmates began to wear peace symbols, although peace was still an abstract concept to us. We all read the story about Joan and Craig, peace devotees who committed suicide by carbon monoxide poisoning in a garage. We were not old enough to be aware of the first trickle of young men departing.

The first one to gain that awareness was my brother, or perhaps my parents on his behalf. Sometime in the early seventies, this extraordinary television show began to air in which government officials drew draft lottery numbers from a barrel, and my whole family became transfixed by it. As my memory has it—surely, I must be wrong—a studio audience of young men witnessed the drawing and were interviewed for their reactions afterward, although I can't remember or imagine what those reactions could possibly have been. For our part, we were relatively safe; Daniel's number was high, the peak years of escalation over. Still, much as my brother's mind is a mystery to me, Daniel must have toyed with the possibility of going to war and agonized briefly over his responsibility as a citi-zen—a fighting-aged male citizen—and finally struggled with his guilt for having been spared.

When the week of Daniel's graduation came, it brought with it excitement and preparations the like of which I'd rarely witnessed. Mother and I baked and froze hundreds of tiny hors d'oeuvres—mini-quiches, triangles of spinach and feta, creampuffs. Yards of fabric were gathered to skirt the tables, and Mother matched candlesticks to the fabric swatches. Of all the people in my family, Daniel was the one least interested in these goings-on. His final week of high school was consumed by late nights out with friends, followed by sleeping jags that lasted into the afternoons. The only time I heard him discuss the party with Mother, they got into an argument over whether beer would be provided for his friends.

"It's my party!" Daniel protested.

"It's *our* party," Mother countered. "And, in my opinion, you and your friends drink too much beer."

"Look at Dad, the way he sloshes down all those Manhattans. What's the big deal about a couple of beers?"

At that, Mom's temper flared, and she told Daniel he'd better speak respectfully of his father.

"Dad would be on my side, if he were home!"

On that point, I did not doubt Dan. We mostly avoided contention for Dad's sake, and not for Mother's. In the old days, it was one of Dad's few complaints that he was constantly having to tiptoe around in this houseful of sensitive women. Yet I know he was sensitive enough, himself, to be pained by our skirmishes.

Finally, the day of Daniel's graduation arrived. It was, in many ways, an awkward day, and a sad one. Within weeks of the ceremony, several of his classmates would ship out to training camp and, afterward, to fight overseas. More would follow later, though no one knew that day who they would be.

Over in a corner, near the bar, Daniel and his friends slouched, looking ill-at-ease in their suits, their new manhood. After they had a few drinks and mixed with the adults, they appeared eager to move on to less formal surroundings. I watched them as I leaned back against the picnic table, bracing myself with my arms. I had just turned fourteen. I didn't know where I belonged, hanging around with Daniel and his friends or out on the lawn with my parents and their friends. Either place, I was decidedly a third wheel, wrapped like a present in my white eyelet dress. Still, I was glad to be there, and I guess I was happy for my brother.

Daniel's friend Victor started toward me. Suddenly aware of how I must've looked, I blushed and turned away. Usually I remembered to round my shoulders, to hide my newly prominent breasts. I was especially self-conscious around Victor after the ski trip. He wasn't my boyfriend, exactly, but we did spend time together in orchestra, and after the Christmas concert, he'd gotten me to drink sloe gin out in the parking lot with him. How awful it was, syrupy and malignant, like cough medicine. But it had given me a warmth that had flushed my cheeks, a warmth that had allowed me to lean back against his icy car while he pressed into me, probing my mouth over and over again with his tongue.

As I looked away across the lawn to avoid eye contact with Victor, I could see Grandma Katherine in the garden, chatting with one of the neighbors, probably about perennials, and Mrs. Martin, in her sunglasses and brightly-printed sheath, gesturing with her bourbon glass. I knew I would be expected to converse with her. We had our interest in writing in common. She was a columnist for the local weekly.

In truth, I never was comfortable talking with her, for although she was obviously intelligent, she was strangely jocular, laughing at inappropriate moments and acting in an unguarded way the other adults I knew never would have. Maybe that's how she made the adults around her laugh, by startling them.

My mother worked from table to table, lifting the skirts, slowly advancing to where I stood. "Laura," she said when she spotted me, "isn't there anyone you could talk to?"

She didn't wait for me to answer, but instead turned and called for my father. "Honey," she murmured when he came, "we're getting low on some things."

Mrs. Martin, who by now had joined us at the bar, paused in pouring her bourbon. "My car's parked out on the street. Would you like me to run out?" She winked at me. "Laura could come to keep me company."

"Well . . ." my mother said and then hesitated, frowning. "It would help if you could. A case of beer, a fifth each of whiskey and scotch, and two of gin I think would do it." Then she scurried inside to fish out the money.

Mrs. Martin was socially prominent, but with her skull-hugging dark cap of hair, her bright dress, and her violently red-orange lipstick, she seemed to me the kind of woman other women like to keep their eyes on. I watched her carefully as we pulled out onto the road, imagining she was a recently released mental patient whose hair had only just started to grow back in after brain surgery. Her driving disconcerted me with its abrupt stops and starts; I found it difficult to give my attention to the conversation we were having.

"Why don't you call Millie Rogers, over at the Bulletin?" Mrs. Martin asked. After a sudden turn, we had jerked to a stop in the parking lot, a few inches shy of the building's brick side wall. Mrs. Martin turned and gave me a smile. Flecks of lipstick marred her front teeth. "I hear she hires high school students as interns over the summer."

"Thanks for telling me," I said. I pictured Millie Rogers in my mind's eye, from the photograph which ran above her column.

I wanted Mrs. Martin to tell me everything she knew about Millie Rogers, like how old she was, and how she'd gotten her job at the paper, but instead she asked me, "Now, why didn't you go off tonight and have some fun with your brother and his friends?"

I was spared having to answer because Mrs. Martin was distracted by the liquor store cashier counting out her change. But after we returned with our rattling load of packages, she pushed me for a response. "I would have given my eye teeth to have an older brother like yours when I was a girl. With all the friends of his who must hang around . . ." She raised one of her penciled-in brows.

I didn't like the way the car seemed to pitch too abruptly for the curves as we drove the highway back. More than once, I felt the wheels go off onto gravel and, looking to Mrs. Martin for a reaction, saw none. The landmarks went by, one by one, distorted by my distance from them. Mrs. Martin, oblivious to my growing fright, went on about her girlfriend's brother and how he'd introduced her to so many beaus. "He was the one I'd really had a thing about all along," she confessed, "but it wasn't until I was in college that we slept together."

I released my grip on the arm rest and turned to stare at Mrs. Martin. Had she really said what I thought I just heard? Then I heard the brakes squeal, looked up, saw that we were in the oncoming lane.

"Pull back over!" I screamed. The moment seemed to pass slowly, and I remember taking a good, long look at Mrs. Martin, thinking how ironic it was that I would

spend the last few seconds of my life with her. The image
of her lipstick-marred teeth burned into the back of my
eyes. I thought with regret about my mother, Dad,
Grandma Katherine, even my brother, none of whose
faces appeared to me just then.

After the impact, I was overpowered with sensations
from inside my body. It felt like I was drowning in blood.
Gradually, I let in the fragmented light from the street
lamp. I realized the person who had been screaming off
in the distance was me.

MY RECOVERY WAS LONG AND SLOW. I watched the summer pass through gauze bandages. Everyone did their
best not to say much about how I looked. I knew without
their telling me that the stitches across my forehead made
a Frankenstein out of me. I had a number of fractures.
One leg, in particular, had been crushed, and the bone
was held together by a metal pin.

When I asked Mother about Mrs. Martin at the hospital, I was told only that she'd suffered a concussion and
had been discharged the day after the accident. Later, I
found out from Grandma Katherine that Mrs. Martin had
tried to phone me. Because she hadn't met with success,
she had written me a letter. My mother, upon opening it,
must have read the signs of Mrs. Martin's imminent
breakdown in the letter's frenetic prose, its missed logic.
Mother didn't pass it on to me. And two weeks later,
about the time I was to be released from the hospital,
Mrs. Martin signed herself into a private clinic for a summer's stay.

Surprisingly, the person most horrified by what had
happened was Daniel. He was at my bedside every day,

offering to do me favors, to run errands to the library and to the stationery store. Daniel brought his friends home to visit me, until I admitted I was too vain to let them see me anymore. He was even reasonably civil to my friends Melanie and Joanne. The connection between my accident and Mrs. Martin's drinking was not lost on him. He wasn't making any promises about sobriety in college, but all summer long he swore off beer drinking. Nor would our father's drinking pass without comment. Not that Daniel's pestering seemed to affect Dad. If anything, Dad seemed to be drinking more that summer than I remembered from past summers. Saddened and worried by my accident, and perhaps by other things, he sometimes came to the dinner table overly emotional and even weepy—a sure sign that he'd been to the cupboard several times to refill his glass.

An uneasiness spread through our house that summer as, one by one, Daniel's classmates readied themselves for college or conscription. Grandma Katherine tried to distract me from the tense atmosphere. She played endless card games with me up in my room to pass the slow hours of my convalescence. Melanie introduced Joanne and me to backgammon. Victor stopped by with flowers and gadgets and promises of tennis games toward the fall when I was feeling better. I was glad for the attention, but none of it dispelled the household's underlying conflict.

One day I was passing the landing from which stairs led up to Katherine's apartment when I heard voices and paused to listen. Mom was up there with Katherine. "The driveway was blocked, so we couldn't have gotten a car out," she was saying. "I don't know why you have to be so critical. It isn't helping anything at this point."

"Daniel or one of his friends could have gone out to the store. They had cars."

Mother nearly wailed, "Can't we just drop it?"

"How?" Katherine screamed back. I heard the antique rocker that Mom had recently bought as a gift for Grandma Katherine scrape across the floor. "How could you have risked your daughter's life with that, that lush? Dammit, Kate, I'm so angry with you, I could, I could—"

I could see them from where I stood. Grandma was shaking with anger. "Get out of here, Kate," she screamed. "I don't want your things in here, either."

Grandma Katherine shoved the rocker down the stairs. My mother stood still, with her mouth held slightly open. Her face had lost all its color. She turned away from her mother and started down the stairs. At the bottom, she stepped gingerly over the chair, without looking down at it.

My mind urged a hopeless equation: if the chair was undamaged, they'd make up with each other. Later, brushing the splintered wood with the tips of my fingers, I felt vaguely responsible what had happened.

Holding the broken rungs and spindles in one hand, like pieces of tinder wood, I hobbled down to the cellar. It took another trip to rescue the chair. I laid the rocker down on the dusty, paint-splattered surface of Dad's workbench, and studied it under the loud fluorescent light. I felt so torn inside, looking at the graceful turns and the darker hue of varnish in the creases, a beauty I believed could not be salvaged. I sobbed and sobbed over the ruined chair, as if it was one of the women who had broken.

I stood a long time in the cellar, waiting for my father to come so that I could hold the injured wood up to him, because I had hoped he could restore everything.

MY LEG WAS SO WITHERED when they finally took the cast off, I found it difficult to imagine it supporting me. Little by little, my strength returned. I stumped around on one crutch, gradually putting more pressure on my healing leg. There were still the long afternoons spent reclining on the sofa, when Victor, if he wasn't working, came to play parcheesi or chess with me. Mostly, we talked. At first, about the music we enjoyed in common. We agreed that Beethoven's Seventh was terrific and that the time our classmates Debbie Parma and Peter Schukovsky played Bach's Concerto in D for two violins, the sound—our hearts!—had risen above the plebian for a time.

Later in the summer, we moved on to other topics. His parents were divorcing, and their constant battling was wrenching him apart. He looked forward to his first semester away at Cornell.

In the meantime, I worked on strengthening my leg. On doctor's orders, my dad drove me to the town pool for synchronized swimming practice three days a week. Dad had first taught me to swim, giving me a gentle push as he let go, watching after me as I sputtered and then my strokes took hold. Dad loved to swim, though he did so with prodigious slowness, pausing at the end of each length to catch his breath and hike his madras swim trunks. We used to make a game of it, seeing how many lengths I could swim for each one of his.

After my accident, though, it was difficult to trust that I could kick, even with my weight borne up by water. I moved with only my arms at first, using my good leg whenever a leg was necessary to steady my stroke. Gradually, I got used to pushing my injured leg against the water's resistance. Thanks to the swimming, by the time Victor came by for our last visit before he went off to college, my two legs were identically tanned and muscled.

I didn't wait for Victor to come up to the house. Instead, I ran out to his car with my tennis racquet in hand for the promised game.

When we parted, he told me, "I'll be back, Laura, you bet I'm coming back." And then he leaned over and kissed me, a chaste yet lingering kiss.

When he did come back to visit Felicity over Thanksgiving, he didn't want to talk much about himself. He wanted to catch up on what was happening in town. We had talked before about the draft and our opposition to the war. We didn't talk about it then. Even though college deferments were being phased out and Victor had a low lottery number, I hardly imagined that he would be called to active duty. The war was winding down.

Victor and I parked down on the school service road so we could make out together. Devoted as we had become to these routine sexual explorations—and as blissfully as our bodies hummed together—I didn't think either of us had our hearts in it. I had the idea he might be going out with someone else and didn't mind, really. I was still glad for his company.

Victor was called up for military service the following week. But I wasn't immediately aware of what had happened, and by the time I found out, he had already reported for basic training. Depressed as he might have been by the turn his life had taken, Victor was not one to shirk what he saw as his responsibility. His letter to me made that clear. Soon he would ship off to Vietnam, and without my having seen him again. His body would be flown back in May, about the time my brother Daniel returned from his first year in college.

5

WHEN I WAS IN MY TEENS, Grandma Katherine and I used to speak a secret code of literary names like Mrs. Dalloway and Father Latour, which disconcerted Mother, because they were names she herself had forgotten. She had no way of making the connection, and we didn't help by giving clues. That same feeling of conspiracy strikes me as we stand in Katherine's apartment this morning, surveying the chaos, the half-filled boxes. The books—any of them that are salvageable—are mine. Grandma Katherine has just told me so. I am bent over one of the boxes, exclaiming over the contents, trying to mask a hint of sadness in my voice. Then, there Mom is. The Chekhov volume I had rooted for so eagerly a few seconds ago suddenly feels weighty in my hand. I notice it smells faintly of smoke. My mother's presence dulls my happiness—and more so, I can see, Grandma Katherine's.

I am already broken-hearted that Grandma Katherine no longer has any need for the books. Believing that Mother has never had the need—and never will—makes me sadder yet. Behind Grandma's attention to my literary gifts was always her unspoken assumption that she and I shared a joy that had passed my mother by. Seeing Mother surrounded by books, I want to question that assumption now. I feel the truth about her is bound to be more complex.

"I see Katherine has told you about the books," Mother says. "It would be nice if you could take them with you when you go."

Already, I have thought of that. I've thought of what fine company the books will make as I drive through the bleak scenery of northern Ohio. It will be like taking a piece of home back with me, the part I have missed. Maybe the apartment I plan to move back to won't look so empty after all. If I use books to fill in spaces, they might muffle Dennis's absence. Otherwise, what? What will I find to do with those bare green walls? Everything I want to keep—the Oriental silkscreens, the botanical drawings—is not mine, but ours. All I solely possess is a dusty set of Munch prints, which I had planned to throw out. I can't understand how I had borne looking at them before.

Perhaps it's the shock of having a big city newspaper thumped on my doorstep every morning, with its foreign policy analysis and police blotter reports, after having been raised in a small town. Or maybe it's recent events in the Middle East—the hostage-taking, the shouting hysterical mobs of people who remind me of nothing so much as the flagellants I read about in Barbara Tuchman. Something has roused me to a state of alarm, so much so that when Dennis and I were together, one topic of conversation we returned to was: if the first strike went out, how would we get from where we were to some meeting place so that we could go down together into a shelter or, at the least find each other, so we could die together?

But the reality is that so far I've survived everything that has happened to me, as I will no doubt survive

Grandma Katherine. Someday, when I least expect it, I will receive a long distance phone call about her. My parents will tell me, "There's nothing you can do," but I'll face a hard choice. Will it make a difference whether I am with her when she finally does depart from me? And to whom would it matter? To me? To her?

I turn to Mom. "The books will fit in my car."

"I hope so," she answers. "I'd like to see them out of this house."

I wait until we are out of Grandma Katherine's earshot before I ask, "What's the hurry?"

"There's a lot of cleaning up to do, and we'll have to move things out of here. Come on, you really ought to have a look. I don't want you to think I'm sending her away without a reason."

How well my mother knows me.

Like a child anticipating a surprise, I allow myself to be led, and I keep my head lowered until we are standing in the center of the room. The air reeks with the intrusive, discordant scents of an unkempt stove. I squeeze my eyes shut, then open them again. Intense sunlight pulses through the thick sheets of plastic which cover the hole where there once had been a ceiling. Grandma Katherine's kitchen is unrecognizable as such now. The floor is streaked dark, heaped with dust and cinders. Layers of wallpaper have peeled away, revealing the ugliness beneath, the house's charred, dead bones.

Mother and I stand still, both straining to picture the room as it was before.

"Dad says you and Grandma Katherine were the only ones home when the fire broke out," I say.

"Yes," Mom replies. "I was downstairs, quilting and watching TV. After a while, your grandma came down the stairs and joined me. It's a show she usually listens to, but that evening, she seemed anxious. She kept on moving back and forth, with her arms wrapped around herself. I thought she might be cold, and tried to share the quilt with her, but she couldn't sit still and I couldn't get anything done. So I went on upstairs to fetch her a sweater.

"I smelled the smoke before I saw anything, and it was thick, but I ran through it up the stairs. All I had to to do was stick my head around the corner to see that something in the kitchen was burning. I don't know what made me do it, but I ran downstairs and grabbed the fire extinguisher, then ran back up again. I emptied out the whole thing, thinking there was maybe still a chance I could put it out, but the flames kept coming back.

"Of course, I dialled the fire department then, and Mother and I went to wait out by the road. She was hysterical—crying out and lifting her hands to her face—and I can tell you, that's just about how I felt inside. There was nothing in the world we could do but just stay right where we were and wait, seeing how much of the house was going to burn up before they got here. You'd be amazed how the glow lit up the sky."

"Then Dad came, right?"

"Just after the fire trucks. Somebody had gotten word to him. One of the neighbors, I suppose."

"And now, what are you going to do up here?" I ask.

My mother sighs. "I suppose it'll just revert to what it was before, attic storage. Do you remember it, back before we remodeled? The attic was your favorite place to play. Oh, my, that seems long ago."

Something in her tone of voice makes me look up, and I catch my mother in an arrested gesture. Almost as if she were about to reach over, to ruffle my hair.

"I remember," I say. And, somehow, memory does transmit a faint picture of her bending over, assisting me with something, along with a sense of the intensity with which we used to relate to each other. If she smiled on me, I was goodness; but if she turned her back, I ceased to exist. It occurs to me, glimpsing the two of us in the quiet of being alone together, that it is a room we will someday reenter.

AFTER MOTHER HAS GONE BACK DOWNSTAIRS and I have returned to the task at hand, my eye catches on a patch of red near the top of one of the boxes. I let out a little cry and kneel down there. "Grandma," I say, "do you remember reading *Silences* together?"

Yes, I can see by the look on her face that she does. I am relieved she has not forgotten, and then I feel a wave of sadness. The title had a literal meaning for her. It referred to all those years she had sat, silenced, in awe of my grandfather. And then there was her unexpressed envy for his position. A small voice within her ached to cry out: *a professor! Why, I read and think as much, myself!* As a matter of fact (which she only revealed to me later, by accident), my grandfather had developed a habit of passing on the books he read to her, and soliciting her opinions on them. More than a few times at a dinner party, she had kept silent while others praised her husband for her idea.

Silences unleashed decades of her indignation, and she had become, at least in private, a more ferocious woman.

Even my mention of the book still awakens her determination. It is good to see a trace of that spirit in her, good that there is enough feeling left to bring out the sharpness in her face.

"Hand it to me," Grandma Katherine demands. But then her face softens as she handles the book, using her fingertips to trace over the stamped, sunken letters which spell out the title. She smiles faintly, as if she is not quite sure of her own conclusion. She says, "Maybe I forced it on you. This book couldn't have possibly meant as much to you as it did to me."

"It did," I said, "because—remember?—you warned me that things hadn't changed as much as we wished they had, and what you said was true."

Grandma Katherine lays the book aside. "I don't doubt you're going to do well, just the same."

She touches my hand with a gnarled one of hers. The touch feels cloying, and I want to draw away. Like Dennis, she burdens me with her belief. I wish I could tell her something simple—that I am happy, or that I've succeeded.

I walk in between two rows of packed cartons. The space is closed and crowded where it had been open and spacious before. Any moment, Grandma Katherine might ask me about graduate school, and I'm not going to be able to answer her. If only Grandma had been the one to go. If only. But with that thought, I'm wishing my own mother out of existence, and with her, myself.

"School's not so easy." I sigh. "Maybe you would have done better. Writing about literature takes all the joy out of it." I study Grandma's upturned face. How can I tell her I may not be cut out to be a graduate student?

"You did fine last year," Grandma Katherine observes. "So, one project doesn't work out. It's not too late to begin another."

"Last year was more like a continuation of undergraduate, with lectures and seminars, but now we've come to a point where it all boils down to advancing my own agenda. And I'm not sure I know what that agenda is. I only know that what I'm studying doesn't speak to me. I seem to be interested in things no one else has heard of. The standard stuff—the canon—I can't write about. The reactions that strike me as true are all considered beside the point. I can't make it out. The professors' reactions seem so arbitrary. For the first time in my life, I've run up against a wall. There's no way to please them."

I'm thinking about my Grandpa Schrier, wondering if I would have displeased him, too.

"Don't start running yourself down. You're sounding like your mother," Grandma Katherine says sharply.

I feel like crying and hanging my head. I want Grandma Katherine to hug me and comfort me. But I've seen Grandma Katherine with my mother, and don't trust that her sympathy will be broad or deep enough for me.

Why should I hang my head, anyway? Why should any of the three of us?

Grandma Katherine does her best to stare at me, even though she cannot see. Her expression is strangely exaggerated, now that she has no perception of how she appears.

She is standing near a window, so that the light reveals a shimmering pinprick of moisture near the corner of her mouth. I can see even the faintest white hairs, which soften her cheeks and her stubborn, outthrust jaw, and the upright creases like a row of tiny paper cuts, scoring the flesh above her mouth. I remember Mother's comment that those creases come from frowning. Coming from her, the remark seemed like only another portion of bitterness. Never, for the whole duration of my childhood, did I ever trust either my mother or my grandmother to speak unbiased truth about each other.

I sink down to the floor between the cartons of books. I can't recall having had all that much difficulty with the books and stories I'd read while I was still at home. Has literature changed that much, or have I? I can no longer easily identify with characters. I pull back, to "catch" the detachment. From the first, I generally disliked whatever was "in" with other literature grad students. Not that I wasn't drawn into it at the same time. I was, and it was an odd, fatalistic attraction. As I read, I could feel my own emotions go brittle and fall away.

"The stories I've read lately are all about people who long for intimacy, but can only manage to hold onto it for brief moments," I say.

She seems suspicious. "Estrangement," she remarks, "that's nothing new."

I feel the odd sensation of having a blind person see right through me. "It's new in the sense that it hasn't been written about in quite this way," I say defensively.

"For this family, there's nothing new about estrangement. We wrote the book on it."

I rest my elbows on my knees. "I always thought you were happy, except occasionally with Mom. And I don't remember that we were distant with each other. I look back on the times we spent as close ones. In fact, I'll be honest with you—it hurts me to hear you describe it that way."

Katherine's face falls, and she looks momentarily flustered, as if I have caught her doing something dishonest or self-serving.

"Don't you remember the day we drove all the way into Buffalo to hear John Cheever give a reading?" I ask her. "And how we got a flat tire and had to change it on that bridge that crosses over the steel mill? All those cars flying by, splattering us with slush and wet cinders?"

"Oh, yes." Katherine smiles, faintly. "We should have taken it as a sign to turn back."

"Why? It worked out beautifully. Remember, when we tried to sneak in late, how he said something droll? Then later, he sought us out at the reception. He made quite a fuss over the fact that you were going back for your masters."

"That was because he knew my husband."

"Just barely, Grandma. He was interested in you. Oh, I remember it as a wonderful afternoon—one of the first times I'd felt as if my world had expanded. When I think of all the things I've done with you, Grandma . . ."

"But that was years ago," Grandma Katherine reminds me.

"I guess it was," I say, and for a moment, silence moves in to fill the space between us.

"Anyway, it doesn't matter, does it?" I say. Even if it was years ago. It happened. We saw John Cheever. We existed then, didn't we? I'm not saying that I remember the times I spent at this house as being perfect. In fact, I remember with great clarity how I ached to get away, to escape from the confinement of this family and this little town. Yet, I was also happy here. The world seemed to revolve around me. I'll never forget what a shock it was to move away from here, and to find out it didn't.

"Part of the reason I came back now, you see, was because I remember the way we were, once. I was coming back to something I remember as good. Because it seems I can't manage to do anything right in my life now. I hate graduate school—and I don't know if I'm going to be able to stick it out. And something has gone wrong between me and Dennis. I'm so sorry, I hate to be telling you these things."

There. I have bared myself to her. I look across for her reaction.

With her dusty hand, Grandma Katherine reaches and touches my forearm. I feel relieved to be looking up to her once more, if only for a moment. I feel comforted. She exhales softly. "I know it's hard for you to see it that way. But you'll come out of it all right. You've got a good head on your shoulders."

I let go of my own breath and stare at her. It's a relief to be able to confess to her, a relief I hadn't expected.

Then she squeezes my arm, hard, with more strength than I thought she had left.

I turn away from Grandma Katherine now, turn away from so much feeling, and look out the window. A cabbage butterfly has found its way up to us and settled lightly on the sill. It must be surprised to have attained such a height. I watch as the butterfly tentatively parts its wings and tests the gentle current of air. I see how fragile its wings are, how much like Grandma Katherine's papery hand. How quickly her grip can go limp. How quickly her mind turns from that pinprick of happiness and light, back into its own dimness. Life is only a series of moments now, brief moments for which she summons herself.

The years we've spent together in this house are part of a past—only fragments are left, held together by the thin string of my memory. Dennis, too, already seems lost to me. I see him in a series of movie stills, brief postcards of sensation. And although they seem too bright at first, too hurtful, I can imagine them fading.

Outside, the butterfly beats its wings a few times and takes off like a glider on the breeze. I watch with a kind of longing as it grows smaller and more distant, until it is no more than a spot of light.

Why is it so easy for me to let Dennis and Grandma Katherine exit my life, as if our connection had been accidental in the first place? Why is it I can view them at such a distance?

When Mother has returned with the packing tape, we work together, sealing the boxes shut. The air is stale and sullen, as if we are sealing tombs. Katherine faces the window, and I feel that we have lost her.

I study my mother's face. Gone is the opaque expression she had worn like a shield against Grandma Katherine for so many years. To her, I suppose, this room stands as a monument to the fact that she has failed her mother in some essential way, and that her mother has failed her in return. It is a malignancy, with its scarred walls and blistered countertops, right there in the center of our house. I see Mother reach to touch one of the walls. Her hand comes away blackened. She contemplates the soot on her fingers. And I think I understand, for the first time, her need to paint and paper over things, to keep them concealed.

Mother does her best to act lighthearted, even cheerful. She bustles around the room and makes a few half-hearted attempts at whistling. She pauses to brush a strand of hair back or to re-tuck her blouse, bestowing an absent smile on no one in particular. I watch her strained charity with a curiosity I have often felt toward her.

"I remember reading this back when I was in school," she says tentatively, touching the spine of a book. Her voice sounds wistful.

There is a certain grace, and a sadness, in her mention of the past. At these moments, her eyes go blue and reflective, and there's an unmasked, disarming beauty about her.

"I once thought I'd be a teacher," Mom says, so quietly I might have missed it.

She has never told me this before. "Why didn't you?" I ask.

"I don't remember." Mom sighs.

"Don't remember! How can you not remember something that must have been that important to you?"

"Well, I know my parents didn't especially encourage me. They thought if I taught, it ought to be at the university level. But that's not what I wanted."

"What did you want?"

"Oh, to teach younger children. At most, high school level."

"And they didn't approve?"

"No. And by then, I'd met your father. I wasn't interested in pursuing it anymore."

"Not because of Dad. Because of what you wanted," I say.

Mother is losing her patience with me. "I guess!" she says. "What difference does it make now? Before you know it, I was married and busy with you children. I had forgotten about the whole thing."

LATER, AS I STAND WITH MOTHER AND GRANDMA on the landing, Mother makes light conversation, perhaps to draw herself away from introspection. I cannot look up the short flight of wooden stairs without thinking of how the rocking chair came thundering down, shattering into ugly debris at our feet. But Mother chats hopefully about the library of tapes Grandma Katherine will have use of in the nursing home, and ticks off a list of creature comforts she has packed.

"Is there anything else you can think of?" Mother asks.

Grandma Katherine grips the banister.

I add my own suggestions, and infuse enthusiasm for my mother's thoughtfulness. It seems the excited tone in our voices is encouraging to Grandma Katherine. She lets go of the banister and gravitates closer to us. Receptiveness loosens the clenched fist of her face.

"Oh, there's something I almost forgot!" Mom exclaims, and bounds over to the closet.

I touch Grandma Katherine's hand, lightly, and ask her, "Are you feeling all right? I don't feel quite right myself, to tell the truth."

Grandma Katherine says nothing but smiles slightly. Once again, I see the moisture appear at the corner of her mouth. Like babies do, she blows a small, soundless bubble.

Mother returns carrying a small wooden model of our house. Amazed, I stroke the miniature planked siding. The intricacy of the thing makes it seem almost magical, and I want it for myself.

"Daniel made this for you, Mother. It's a model of our house," Mom explains. She takes Grandma Katherine's hands and forms them around the model. Then, with a squeeze, she lets go. As Katherine caresses the model, I watch her struggle for comprehension.

I am impressed by my brother's craftsmanship, impressed that he would have thought to do this himself. Mom is visibly proud of her son.

Grandma Katherine only frowns. "Daniel?" she asks. Her vacant, blue-gray eyes remind me of craters on the moon.

Mother's face turns pale. "Daniel's your grandson, Mother. He's Laura's brother."

"Laura, yes." Grandma Katherine smiles. "And where's Ken? Did he do all this packing?"

I speak up. "Of course not! Mom—I mean, Kate—is the one who did all the work."

Grandma Katherine turns the model over in her hands. "Well, of course," she explains to herself, "Kate's only a housewife. Ken works."

I can see Mother's hands trembling at the ends of her long arms. "I run my own business, Mother. And Ken doesn't work at anything. He's been dead for twenty years."

In a perverse sense, I'm curious about what will be said next. But I don't want to hear it, and wish to forget their whole history and my connection to it. Most of all, I'm horrified over Grandma's loss of reality.

"Why is it," Mother says, "no matter what I've done, or how I've tried to please you, it's always been Ken you've loved? What made me such a great disappointment? I've never figured it out."

Grandma Katherine blinks, and then turns toward my mother's voice. I recognize the emptiness beyond her glazed eyes. She isn't here, not here with us.

Mother presses Katherine for a response, "Oh, Mother, you know I always looked up to you, but you were so . . . formidable. I didn't want to disappoint you."

Tears have formed in Mother's eyes, but she wipes them away defiantly, like a child rubbing away sleepiness, and brings her chin up to a higher level.

"A waste of a college education, that's what you once said. But Kenny was the one who wasn't going to make it. He wasn't serious enough. You were the only one who failed to realize . . . but you'll never see that side of him, so what does it matter?"

Mother fumbles in her pocket for a tissue, and then shields her face with her hand. She looks so vulnerable— so tragically lovely with her downcast waves of golden hair, with her slender, gold and diamond-studded hand which presses at her temples as if to suppress some unwanted truth—that I hesitate to approach her.

I long to say, *What about Daniel? Can't you see, you've done the same thing with me and Daniel?*—but I can't. There's no point in spelling out the truth to someone if they can't see it.

After a deep breath, Mother looks up into Grandma Katherine's face. "It wouldn't have been much of a loss to you, would it, if I had died instead of Ken?"

Then Mother lunges the few steps over to me, lays the weight of her head on my shoulder, and sobs. The gesture is unlike her—usually, she would have stalked away and cried alone—and I am taken by surprise. For, unthinkingly, I have reached to stroke her hair. It feels so like mine, in its heft and in its somewhat sticky texture, that the realization is shocking. I hold my hand still for an instant, weighing the familiar versus the unfamiliar, the self versus the other. But then tears rush into my eyes and I am blurred, myself.

6

WHEN WE COME OUT OF DOORS and into the sunlight, Grandma Katherine squints, as if the brightness is too acute. I wonder how much she can sense in the way of light. Is it like piano music playing dimly in another room? How much is actually perceived and how much is merely remembered?

For Grandma Katherine, who lived so many years as part of the existence of her husband, it must seem as if the world is closing down just when it was beginning to open. I imagine the unutterable sorrow she must feel to hear the papery brown, lifeless leaves drift down through the sky, knowing there are other springs to come, and also knowing that she will not see them. The leaves are slicked down by late fall rains and early sleets, losing their last bit of color as they're ground into the graying sidewalks, the tired soil. The energy is gone, pushing toward new shoots. All that's left is a faint, mortal odor.

Inside the car, Grandma Katherine sits straight and erect. Tears have dried in the corners of her eyes. I try not to cry, myself. Already, this day, I have experienced too many emotions, and I'm afraid if I let them come too readily, they may blunt what I see. The car cruises down Main Street, beneath twin aisles of maple trees. Dad has slowed to accommodate his sense of ceremony, the way one slows for certain festivities: for wedding marches and parades, for funerals.

Familiar landmarks pass by too quickly, before I've had a chance to access what I feel for each and every one. I have to take them as a whole, like a tourist would: the aging clapboard houses, the glass-fronted shops, the dusty vehicles and drooping, golden trees. Somehow, between the trees and the midday sun, it's as if a fine, golden dust has been sprinkled over the town. Despite the houses that need painting, and the soap-smeared windows of shops gone out of business, something has softened the scene for me. For the first time, I feel moved by the sights of Felicity, as if its injuries could be mine.

As we drive out of town, faced by the broad expanse of fields and the well-kept farms, and by the suggestion of hills in the distance, I remember the prediction my friend Joanne once made. She said she knew that I would be able to leave Felicity, because I could see it as a landscape. Joanne knew how distant, how detached I could be. I looked, she said, as if I was trying to memorize everything in preparation for going away.

The highway to Franklin runs straight for long stretches, through farms built on the lake's silt bed. The land is fertile and flat, except for the occasional valley with its modest, winding stream. Agriculture is intensive and evident everywhere, from the low, modern silhouettes of Felicity Cooperative Greenhouses to the hand-lettered billboards boasting strawberries, U-pik-it corn, and LOOK, EGGS!

In the spring, rows of white, bonnet-like cloches poke up from the musty, dark soil. In June, the air is filled with the stench of ripe cabbage, and passersby mob the well-stocked fruit stands on foot and in cars. By midsummer, when the sun is high and the corn is lush, sprinklers wield their crystal whips over the fields in arcs, like droning overseers, for as far as the eye can see. The colors of the fields begin to bronze sometime in August. Today the fields are already stripped bare, clean-furrowed, except for the stipples of corn and of straw. Pumpkins and fancy gourds and bushels of squash ring the produce stands, but soon these, too, will be gone. And I shiver when I remember this place in winter, a desert landscape of wind and shifting snow.

Slowly, the car ascends the blacktopped drive before what appears to be a Tudor castle. Junipers drape their prickled arms close to the car, close enough almost to scratch it. Dad pulls in behind a taxi stand. I am glad to see that the place appears civilized, and that it allows some mode of escape.

Inside, the lobby is not as drab as I feared it would be. Sunlight forces its radiance through a network of tiny windows, and the waxed, sand-colored floor reflects it back on us. Dad and I each grip one of Grandma Katherine's frail arms as we wait before the reception table. A woman with swollen legs stumps by on a walker. The black rubber tips of the walker resemble, in some ludicrous way, her high, black orthopedic shoes.

I lead Grandma Katherine up to her room, which also turns out to be light, if not spacious. Her eyebrows rise, instinctively, as we enter through the open door. Impatiently, Grandma shakes off my hand and propels herself smack into the bed. If my mother were here, this would make Grandma angry, but with me, she laughs.

More cautiously, now, she begins to explore the room. She passes her hands over the whole length of the nubby bedspread before encountering first the smooth wood of the headboard, then the nightstand on the right-hand side.

"For your books," I suggest. "You can read before going to bed."

Grandma Katherine looks up, gives me a shy smile. "Maybe," she says.

She feels her way down the opposite walls, smoothing her fingertips along a bureau, a desk. I brush past her, to look out the window. Below me is a park-like scene, drooping evergreens and a well-kept lawn, which I describe as she approaches. "They're wasting a beautiful view on you," I tell her.

"Oh, I don't know," she says. "I'm glad to hear it's there."

"Maybe you could take some walks down there."

"I doubt it." The skin above her upper lips tightens. She flails with her arm until she locates a chair, then she lets herself down heavily in it. There is so little left to her in the way of flesh that she hardly makes a sound. "I'm getting to be an old lady, you know," Grandma Katherine remarks.

"No, you aren't, Grandma," I answer, because it's my reflex to deny this.

But she ignores me. She heaves a sigh and says, "I suppose I'm going to die here."

I don't know what to say in reply to such an assertion. If only I could look at her from a distance, I could see that what she is saying is probably true.

She takes my hand. "I'm not afraid," she says.

"You used to be," I hear myself say.

"Yes," she admits softly. "I was."

"What is it that's changed?"

I regret the question the moment I ask it. After all, isn't it obvious? She is old and frail, her body is used up. I need to know, and I meant to ask her: *How have you learned to accept the loss?* I still envision her flying between the rows of orchard trees.

"It helps me that I've done some things I'd hoped to do. Or, at least, that I've had a taste of them. But I was surprised to find that what I wanted, well—it wasn't what I had wanted in the first place."

"You mean, like taking the master's?" My voice has gone shrill. I hear myself straining to understand.

"It meant a great deal to me to be able to do the work for myself. I needed to know that I could read, and think, and write myself. I had lived with literature all my life, through Charles." Grandma Katherine traces a circle delicately, thoughtfully on the tabletop, using her finger.

"But that wasn't the most important thing?"

"No, I'd have to say, it wasn't." Grandma Katherine glances away, like a girl suddenly overcome by shyness. "You were."

"Grandma!" I rush to her and grasp her by the shoulders, but she twists away from me.

"You wanted to know, so I told you."

I recognize this as an apology, as an expression of the difficulty she had in telling me. I've felt the same rectitude on my part. Love, for both of us, is a most uneasy subject. And the contingency of death makes an admission of love only the slightest bit more possible.

A knock rattles the door, and I jump to open it. Dad stands there, burdened with a heavy load of luggage. I snatch a few of the outer pieces to relieve him.

"I'm sorry. We were getting settled, or I would have come downstairs to help," I say.

He sees Grandma Katherine with her head down and her back turned to me. "That's all right," he says. "What you're up to is more important."

"Yes," I say. Grandma turns and smiles faintly, off into the distance beyond the door.

"Here," Dad says to me, extending his arms, and I relieve him of garment bags and of hat boxes, one by one. I lay them carefully out on the bedspread—too much regalia for a dying person.

Stooping, I ask Grandma Katherine how she would like her things arranged. But she is absent again, and waves me away. I go crank the window open, giving her the small gift of imparted breeze. Wiry white tendrils fan out around her face. "You go ahead," she says. "I'm tired."

I stand beside her, watching as her eyes close, and as a remote, passive smile spreads out across her face, her message to me is clear. She has given; now I must give back.

Dad and I empty the luggage and fill the closet and the drawers. The room feels like a skeleton, and we are fleshing out bones. As I place her underthings in one drawer, I think that this is the first time I've even seen them, or touched them. I refold her slips, which are nothing more than a whisper in my hand.

I'm glad for Dad's presence. He and I are silent companions, but we comfort each other in our silence. I no longer can converse well on his subjects—sports and local politics. The familiarity I once had with his interests has worn thin. Whenever I bring up the football season, or the school board election, I'm aware that I can only say so much, and only then if Daniel's not there to call my bluff. Still, my relationship with Dad is more than just a formality. He has comforted me with silence since the first time I cried on his shoulder over a long-eyelashed boy who didn't love me. And back during my teenage years, Dad served as interpreter between Mom and me, negotiating the finer points of truces, a role he has not entirely relinquished.

He pokes his head out from the closet. "Your mother called and left a message at the front desk. She's on her way over. She wanted us to wait until she comes."

"Why didn't she come in the first place?" I say.

Dad glances over at Grandma Katherine, to make sure she isn't paying attention. "You don't need me to tell you that she's always gone out of her way to do things for her mother. Today can't be easy for her."

I take this as a reprimand and feel momentarily chastened. "It isn't easy for anyone," I say defensively. "There's something to be said for those societies who revere their elders. They wouldn't dream of an institution like this; in their society, there are no parallels to it."

Dad doesn't speak right away. Maybe I've offended him with my sharp tongue, my tendency to lecture.

I follow his eyes over to the door. Mom has arrived. Their eyes communicate to each other a sympathy which excludes me.

Dad rests his hand on my shoulder. "Come on," he says, "let's give them a moment alone together."

I look from Kate to Katherine—from mother to grandmother—but I can't see as much of the similarity I had noticed when we were all younger. They both were such proud-looking women. Grandma Katherine was upright, even if she wasn't very tall. Mother inherited Grandma Katherine's long, slender legs. Both had been known to use their beauty as a weapon against the men in their lives. When my mother crossed her legs, tilting her head back to please my father, her kneecap appeared sharp enough to cut through her stockings.

I realize I have grown sharp and slim and—yes—beautiful like my mother, while Katherine has shrunken. It is hard to see myself as one of them. I close the door. Dad and I retreat down the stairs.

He and I walk the grounds. His lips are tight and his jaw is set. He won't say so, but he's angry with me. *Disappointed*, he would say, as if any conflict between us comes from my lack of maturity.

"It was my idea," Dad startles me by saying. "I could see caring for Grandma Katherine was getting to be too much of a burden for your mother."

"Because of her blindness?" I ask.

"That, and other things, too. Kate's done her duty. Twice over, I'd say, considering what a hard time her mother has always given her. She's done a damn sight better than that brother of hers probably would have done. So, if you feel the need to blame somebody for this," my father says, "Blame me, not her."

Anger flushes my cheeks. Neither of us has anything further to say as we return to the building. Dad tours me through the public rooms downstairs. He checks his watch, calculating the correct time for us to reenter Grandma Katherine's room.

MOTHER IS BENDING CLOSE TO GRANDMA KATHERINE, explaining something, when Dad and I enter. Mother leans forward, drawing an envelope from her jacket pocket. She slits open the flap with her sharp index fingernail. Old, discolored photographs spill out onto Mother's lap.

"I brought these for you," she tells Grandma. "They're pictures of the family."

"Really?" Grandma Katherine cocks her head. "Where did they come from?"

Mother comes close to forming a smile. "They're yours. From some of your old scrapbooks. I saw them on your bookshelves and carried them down out of the fire. I couldn't stand the thought of having the past go up in flames and being lost forever."

"Well." Grandma Katherine folds her arms across her chest. "I don't know what good they'll do me, if I can't see them."

I expect to hear the scrape of my mother's chair against the linoleum floor, followed by the sound of her brisk, short footsteps receding down the hall. But she does not rise to leave. She draws in closer to Grandma Katherine, and says, "I realize that, Mother. I was going to describe them to you."

Grandma Katherine sits up slightly in her seat. In a small voice, strangely meek for her, she says, "I'd appreciate that."

"Well, then," Mother says, and smiles. She holds the edge of one of the photographs delicately between her fingertips. "Here's one of the house, dated 1935."

"Our old house, on Harmon Street?" Grandma Katherine leans forward. "Why, in 1935, we had just moved in. What does it look like?"

"It's the same dark brick that I remember, with dark brown shutters. It must be spring, because there's a twig of forsythia and daffodils spaced out across the front of the house. What's different about it is the trees."

"The trees, yes." Grandma Katherine beams. "They were young."

"Just saplings," Mother answers. "And so are you. There you are, clinging to one of them with both your hands. You look so young! The skin's stretched tight across your cheekbones, and you're laughing." I can hear surprise register in Mother's voice. The woman smiling in the picture is someone she has never known.

"Are there any others?" Grandma's voice lifts, hopefully.

"Oh, yes. This one is of you and Father, dancing. You're all dressed up. I've never seen you in a hat like that before. You must be at a wedding or something of that kind."

"Dancing . . ." Grandma Katherine repeats wistfully. "Was there a date written down?"

"1928," Mother reads dutifully. "The year before I was born."

"There were so many weddings that year. Do you recognize anyone?"

"It's just a close-up of you and Dad. But it's a lovely picture. I had forgotten how tall he was, how slender and handsome you both were."

"Yes . . ." Grandma Katherine's voice veers off in a dreamy tangent. "Charles was always a fine-looking man." Her face seems almost to grow more youthful, resembling more the face in the picture. Her eyebrows are raised, and I wonder whether she could be imagining herself back in the muscular cage of his arms.

I had meant to ask Grandma Katherine whether she was ever sorry that she loved Charles. But the answer clearly marks her face. She never was sorry. It was simplistic of me to think that, because she had allowed herself to go on, to keep growing beyond the person he had known and loved, she had stopped loving him. It was simplistic of me not to realize that, before Charles died, she could have been happy in a completely different sense. But here she is: smiling, lost in her remembrance.

Mother draws out another picture. "Look!" she crows. "You've had me. And I couldn't be more than a couple of months old."

Katherine chuckles. "What a chubby, happy baby you were."

Mother's eyes sparkle with appreciation. "Yes, I was fat."

"And to think I had been worried about you spoiling our marriage! Of course, you didn't," Grandma Katherine says, covering Mother's hands her own. "It all comes back to me, those memories of the things we three did together. We took long walks and train rides and worked in the garden. What a terror you were there! Not that we blamed you. It was just that you loved the roses so much, you kept trying to pick them. And I remember your father taking you in a knapsack when he rode on his bike. It was a funny sight: Charles, with those long legs in dark trousers, and you, with your tiny blond head peering out from the bag. We were so happy with you, and with each other. It was a time I think we both wished would never end."

Grandma Katherine looks out in the direction of the window, a small smile still fixed on her face. She does not move her hand. Nor does Mother try to extract herself. Rather, she sits very still, with a crooked smile of her own.

The shadows outside the window have grown longer with the afternoon, and in the park-like place below us, evergreens shade an early dusk. A bank of clouds has lowered the sky and tints the whole landscape blue. It does not feel gloomy, though, just calm—like the sky has been covered by warm, lapping water. The clouds are scalloped just like waves, with cracks of peachy-colored sunlit air like froth. I can imagine them breaking softly against my legs.

The air is warm and static with tiny, drifting glowballs of dust. Grandma Katherine's breath deepens until it begins to catch and snag. Mother glances across at me and slowly withdraws her hand. Dad lifts Katherine onto the bed I've opened. Mom slips off her mother's street clothes and her shoes. I pull the bedclothes over, to cover my grandmother. Soundlessly, we retreat out the door.

"Goodnight, Mother," Mom whispers.

By now, the room has become diffused with the pale blues and pinks of sunset. I take one last look at her, at her pale head nodding in the richly patterned light. I do not say goodnight, as my mother did, or even goodbye. I just pause there, until the narrowing crack of the door has shut her off from me.

THE NEXT AFTERNOON, after a morning spent lounging, Mom and I run errands. When we arrive home, even while we're still on the porch, we can hear that the phone is ringing.

"Laura!" Dennis gasps breathless with anxiety. "I've been trying and trying to get through. I'm glad I've got you."

I quickly have a picture of him as he must be, sprawled across that wrinkled batik bedspread I'd gotten him because he didn't have one and didn't care, with a journal or text book turned upside down to hold his place. Or perhaps he is sorting laundry. I think of his things, still slightly damp, spread around the room, drying, because he has run out of dimes and patience. I strain to hear Tchaikovsky playing—who would have thought it possible I could miss the Tchaikovsky?—but can hear nothing. Is it conceivable that Dennis, like I do, finds some things painful to repeat now that we're apart?

"What makes you think I'd be here?" I ask.

He tells me how he became worried when I didn't answer his calls to my apartment. It depresses me to picture my apartment foyer as he describes it, the tottering little table with my letters and papers spilling over. I had forgotten to make arrangements. I can see how he would have been alarmed by my disappearance.

"Is anything wrong?" he asks. "Or are you just visiting?"

"It's Grandma Katherine," I say. "She's burned down a section of the house because she forgot and left something on the stove. So yesterday we moved her to a nursing home."

"Oh, Laura!"

"No, don't overreact, I suppose I made it sound worse than it is—it's just that it feels so bad. To admit there's nothing I can do, do you know what I mean?"

And right there, on the phone, with my mother probably overhearing, I begin to sob. "I mean, there were all sorts of things, the fire was kind of the last straw."

I'm crying, I'm still crying, but I press the palm of my hand hard against my forehead to make the tearing stop.

". . . even if they hired a nurse to stay with her?" Dennis is saying.

My voice is hard and brittle against the tears. "I think there's something about the insurance. And they're not made out of money, Dennis. I think my father may be having some trouble with the business, and that's not made any better by Daniel coming on now and drawing a salary."

"But if he can bring in new business?"

"But for now," I insist, "it's a drain."

My mother crosses from the refrigerator to the kitchen counter, where I can see her. I wonder if she's managed to hear what I just said.

"Look," I tell Dennis, "thank you for calling and I'm sorry I worried you, but I've got to go."

"How long are you going to be there?" he asks. "I mean, you're missing classes, aren't you?"

"You know, Dennis . . ." I lean my forehead against the cool expanse of wall. "I wish I could tell you, but I really don't know."

My voice sounds remote to me. I hang up the phone. I don't go to my mother, who is bustling around the kitchen with some private agenda, a catering job perhaps. I slip on my jacket and go on outside. To walk. That phone call started me thinking that maybe my family doesn't have all the answers. If I have another idea, there's still time to speak up. I walk briskly through the stiff meadow grass, up the hill and around past the fence and the grapevine that is barren now, though in my childhood it used to produce prodigious clusters of sour reddish grapes. What is different now, I realize, is that I don't just have to witness things, I can act. I'm in graduate school now, but I could work. What's to keep me from sharing an apartment with Katherine, if I made careful provisions?

7

WHEN I WAS GROWING UP and felt too contained inside, there was a place I could go. Just over a block from my house and up to the crest of the hill, was a place where I could look out upon the larger world. From there, the public buildings, the scattered houses, the thoroughfares through town appeared as insignificant. I could see broad swaths of farmland, forest tracts, the watercolor smear of Lake Erie—all beyond Felicity. On a clear day, far off on the horizon, I could even see the city of Buffalo, faintly purple in hue against the sky.

Melanie and Joanne and I passed this high spot often on our way to each other's homes. I can remember standing here at various times with each of my friends, contemplating the city and what it held for us. The city meant something different to us then—it was our future, a promise foretold.

Our existence back then, however, was light-years away from the realities of the city. We roamed to each other's houses on a network of paths through the woods. We pedaled our bikes up the steep hills. Our leg muscles grew so strong we could ride ten miles to the shore of Lake Erie. There we let the brown waves wash up against our legs.

About the most adventurous thing we ever did back then was to play hooky. I'd pretend to miss my bus and run over to the next street, where I took the path that led to Melanie's house. Her parents both worked, so we would spend the day at her house, jogging the circumference of the alfalfa field, baking, watching daytime TV, and talking. We did special exercises that were supposed to enlarge our breasts, and we would pretend to psychoanalyze each other, Melanie focusing on me with her intense, heavily-lidded green eyes.

These activities were Melanie's ideas. I just went along, because if anyone disagreed with her, Melanie could make things difficult. Perhaps because she had always been little and slow to develop—although she had by adolescence more than made up for that, with her braces off and her pale Snow White complexion—she was stubborn, and terribly competitive. If she didn't get her way, she would pout, and her allergies would flare up. Before I opposed Melanie, I asked myself if it was worth the trouble.

Joanne used to play hooky with us, but by high school, she'd given up on our goings-on. She was a forward on the girls' basketball team, and she didn't like to miss a practice. Melanie was too small to play, and I hadn't made the cut.

On a particular day that I recall, Melanie and I played hooky alone. When we had exhausted everything there was to do inside, we went out and circled the bog nearby, keeping our eyes open for frogs and dragonflies. The outdoors distracted me. I stopped thinking about my missed class in history, and let myself be drawn in by the fringe of woods. We walked closer than we had ever dared to the old Hanrahan place, which ever since the Hanrahans had died, was reputed to be, variously, the home of Moonies or a drug den. Places like that, in remote locations, with owners no one ever saw, were often held under suspicion, but the "No Trespassing" signs on the driveway and at the boundary of their woods confirmed our suspicions absolutely. The people who lived in the old Hanrahan place drove motorcycles, the only pair of motorcycles in town. We saw them parked alongside the house and ventured closer to take a look. I turned and studied Melanie's face as we stood there partially concealed by the bushes. She wore the same mask of fearlessness she'd worn earlier that morning when she'd declared that she was about to loose her virginity. I'd thought it an improbable boast, but then Melanie had done many things I wouldn't have predicted. So, who knows?

The first whiff of fear had worn off, and we felt immune. We gradually made our way closer to the house. Melanie wanted to be able to see into the windows.

"We'd better be careful," I warned. "They might be on drugs. People on drugs can be dangerous."

Melanie leaned forward, pressing her nose against the window glass, her hands shielding her eyes against the glare of the sun. "I wonder if they ever hypnotize people."

A voice from below, in the driveway, startled us. A muscular, menacing-looking man in a black tee-shirt, hardware belt, and jeans yelled at us and started to give chase. We scrambled through the brush.

"What is going to happen if he catches us?" I whispered to Melanie.

By then, he was so close behind me I could hear him wheezing. That sound gave me the adrenaline I needed to break loose.

"Damn kids!" I heard him say under his breath. Then he shouted, "You'd better fuckin' git out of here."

But we didn't need him to tell us to get going. Even after we were on the main path, we kept running. It wasn't until we were out of the woods altogether that we stopped, and stood panting.

"He looked like a Hell's Angel," I gasped.

I was shivering. The bright light stunned me. I saw my house, distant but visible, the city spread out far below and, farther still, the lake's uncertain horizon. Then I heard a familiar jangling sound.

"Look," Melanie said, and tugged on my arm.

Grandma Katherine was out walking our dog Goldie, who recognized my scent, and strained at her lead. She wriggled and then, in a burst, broke free. She was crouched, coming for me fast, with her lead dragging behind her, her tail a flag.

"Oh, Goldie!" I said. I wanted to be mad, but the dog was so happy to see me.

Grandma Katherine was less pleased. "Well, what have we here?" she asked, a corner of her mouth twisted up in a funny, ironic smile.

"I can explain," the glib Melanie offered.

I wondered how. My mind was an absolute blank.

"Choir was cancelled, and that gave us two free periods in a row, so . . ." Melanie explained.

I was mortified at having disappointed Grandma Katherine. I held my eyebrows high so I wouldn't cry.

She didn't reprimand us, for which I was thankful, although I suppose in a way, it might have been better if she had. She went back home to get the car while we waited in near silence.

"She isn't going to tell your mom, is she?" Melanie asked.

I assured her Grandma Katherine wouldn't tattle on us. She would just drive us back to school.

The next day as newspaper staff all lounged around in the school newspaper office, Melanie told the story of our adventure, only the man in it was a Hell's Angel for sure—and we had barely escaped his clutches.

"You don't *know* that he's a Hell's Angel," I scolded her.

But her story had been enough to distract the boys from whatever fool game they had been playing. Rob and Jack were always clowning around, fencing with yard-sticks or bowling over the wastecan. Rob came up behind me and began to massage my shoulders. "Hell's Angel's, huh?"

Later, Grandma Katherine asked me what we had been up to in the woods, Melanie and I. I know the reason why she asked. It was because of the fear she must have seen in our faces as we had emerged from the woods. Seeing as she had been the one to rescue us, I thought it was the least I could do to tell her.

Afterward, when I had told her about the Hanrahan place and the menacing man who looked like a Hell's Angel, she pressed me briefly to her chest. "My dear girl," she had said.

I never could bring myself to play hooky again. Or to go back to that house, at least until years later, when the people who lived there had moved away. Whatever extra steam I had, I blew off in the newspaper office or out on the running track after school. I liked Rob and Jack, Russ and Cindy—the whole newspaper gang. They made me laugh; they distracted me.

IT WAS THE FALL OF MY JUNIOR YEAR of high school when Melanie's parents decided they had to separate. This meant that her dad would get to move with his girlfriend into the second story apartment above the floor covering shop. Melanie's mother became a paler version of herself, as if each extra hour of work and each time she had to raise her voice drained her. Melanie was more flamboyant in school, but to me more remote. I began to hate going to her house and having to look out after her needy little brothers and sisters who stared at me with their incredible long-lashed eyes.

How much easier to go out on the driveway and shoot baskets endlessly, than to sit holed up with Melanie in her kelly green and orange bedroom, not knowing what to say.

I was tempted to hang out more often with Joanne. But then her parents suddenly announced they were moving. Her father's plant was closing; he was forced into early retirement and could no longer afford to make the payments on the house. It was inconceivable to me that the woods and the dogs that roamed them, the bridge across the stream that was fringed by wildflowers in spring, could belong to someone else. I thought of the antique car her father had been assembling down in the basement, piece by piece, for years. I couldn't imagine how it could be moved. And what of the stables, and the meadow where I'd had my first encounter with horses?

Joanne, Melanie, and I were ten years old. I remember Joanne, in chaps, boosting Melanie, who was dressed in hot pink pedal pushers, up onto "Beau."

"Nice outfit," Joanne had remarked. "So, have you ever ridden before?"

Melanie made the mistake of claiming she had, back when she'd spent summers with her cousins.

I imagined she'd felt nervous and was lying. There had always been an animosity between Melanie and Joanne.

Joanne yelled, "Giddiyup!" The sound of the slap she gave Beau's backside still rings in my ears.

Beau streaked across the pasture, only stopping long enough to rear up and then charge in another direction. It wasn't long before Beau had thrown Melanie. She landed, of course, in a pile, and although unhurt, she was crying. I felt remorse because I saw it coming.

Joanne was like that. She tested you. And I had passed all the tests she'd ever given me ever since the day we first met at the fringe of her woods. So I was the one who was left to stand by her on that January day when they auctioned off her ponies, one by one. She gave me a horseshoe she had saved for good luck, and she kept one for herself.

At about the time Joanne was adjusting to her modest home, with abbreviated backyard and new high school, we began throwing mixed parties, mostly with the newspaper crew. My parents seemed genuinely relieved to see me with a whole group of friends, rather than just one or two, and they opened our home for a rather tame party. The most eventful happening was Rob's stunt of folding himself into the family room sleep sofa. But then Melanie had a party, unsupervised as were most things that went on at her house in those days. At first, I enjoyed myself. Jack and I joked around, and I talked earnestly with Cindy. But then, the music seemed to call attention to itself, and standing next to the pinned-up sheets, which hid the basement plumbing, I felt forlorn. My awareness of Rob and Melanie over in the corner was something I couldn't, of course, acknowledge, but it felt like a kind of betrayal. We had all been friends, I thought angrily as the music played on and the notes from the guitar fell to prick me, one by one.

I started jogging the paths I'd once frequented with friends, alone now. When Melanie phoned—I took to seeing her less and less—I paced impatiently, wrapping the cord around my waist. Of course, she and Rob were, as she put it, "making it." Not that anyone had to tell me.

I borrowed more of Grandma Katherine's books. I grew tanned and boxy and muscular waiting for that spring to pass. I could run all the way to the lake past the fields of ripening strawberries, bunching onions, and nearly grown peas. The landscape was spread out before me, and I was the one who would be going places, leaving Felicity behind.

I CROSS THE ROAD AND TRAMP THROUGH what used to be a field. Now evergreens have grown up, and I pass through the neighborhood unseen. I cut through the yard of a newly built house, steal past the sandbox, the elaborate swingset, and on into the woods. This is the path I used to take up to Melanie's house. It skirted Joanne's property as well.

Where are the families with all the money to buy these big new houses coming from? What became of the families, like those of my friends, who have been displaced?

Of course, I know Melanie's mother is living with her younger children in an apartment complex on the edge of the city. And Melanie's father lives with his girlfriend in a rented house in town. Joanne's parents, whom I really could have imagined getting divorced—what with their

clashing exotic tastes—are living together, but in another
town. I haven't hiked this path in years, except in winter,
with skis strapped on. In fact, it's hard to find the path
without the snowmobiles buzzing through, and I lose it a
couple of times.

I've wandered off into a particularly gloomy patch of
hemlocks—the kind of place where no light ever shines,
which a young child would recognize as a witches' haunt.
A St. Bernard bounds through the brush, leaping at me
and barking.

"Come, Roufus, get on out of there! What are you
after?" a loud voice inquires from behind me.

Roufus and I follow the voice. It's about fifty yards or
so back to the path. I'm not sure where I've gone wrong
to have lost my way.

I would never have lost the path through here as a
child. But now the terrain has become strange to me. I
don't have the same access to it I once had. My friends,
too, have over the years lost their presence. They are
reduced to a collection of details. I can no more recall
Joanne's face in my mind's eye than I can reach out and
touch her. But I remember Joanne's monogrammed
oxford cloth blouses, the stiffness of them, how she kept
them in a stack in the drawer. I remember how her wrists
stuck out of the sleeves, bony as my own. I remember the
coolness of her legs as they brushed against mine at night
under her stack of comforters, with the windows wide
open and the winter air streaming in.

I know I've scrambled past these trees with her on our
descent to the creek, where we'd dam off little pools, or
wade, or catch salamanders near the rocks. Imagine if,
just now, Joanne were the one to find me. She always had

the better sense of direction. Only her dog had been a German pointer named Horst.

I don't know if I'd recognize Joanne, because I've only managed to see her once in all the years since we finished high school. She hasn't had an easy time. After high school she ran all the way to Florida to move in with somebody. They broke up and she lost her job, I'm not sure in which order, but I hear from her mom that she's working on her degree again and wants to go on to veterinary school. I'm glad to hear there is something she wants, after all.

And Melanie. Melanie is a lawyer living in Buffalo. On weekends, she sometimes still helps her Mom out with the kids. Over the years, we've drifted apart, and anything I know about her—that she refurbishes antiques, that she has organized a few social events, minor fundraisers—I've heard from someone else. It's not odd, I suppose, that after all those years of having to look out after someone else, to find that she is self-satisfied, well-to-do, and single.

The leaves rustle close behind me, a twig breaks off—I hold my breath, almost believing that either Joanne or Melanie is about to push aside one final branch and appear before me. Instead, a pretty, round-faced young woman with tousled hair pushes her way through the curtain of greenery and bends down to greet the St. Bernard. Then she straightens and looks across at me. "Laura Brunner, isn't it? You don't know who I am, do you?"

I ponder her for a moment, before I admit, "No, I don't."

"Deborah Warner. It's Deborah Johansson now. My husband and I met at school. We live not too far from here—a mile or so in that direction. Our house is one of the ones that looks over the valley."

"Deborah Warner," I repeat. Nothing about the young woman standing before me suggests the slight girl I once knew. She was several years ahead of me in school. We both played the cello, though she had been much better, and had gone on to music school. "You sure have changed."

She tilts her head back and laughs. "Everybody says that."

"Do you still play?"

"Yes, and I taught for a while. But now I've got a little boy, and he keeps my hands full. Except going into the city a couple of evenings a week for rehearsals, that's all. What about you?"

"Still in graduate school." I smile reflexively. By now, some people are beginning to consider my lingering at the university to be a childish evasion of real life. "Well, good to see you. It's been so long since I've walked in these woods, I hope I find my way home."

After I've turned from her, after the sounds of her and the dog have retreated and it's just me scuffing through the leaves, I think back to Deborah. How beautiful and happy she looked. She has lost completely her stunning fragility, that touch-me-not look she wore in high school. In its place is something that makes her seem fuller, more the sort of person I like. And yet, she has chosen the less ambitious path. She had a gift. Her choice puzzles and vaguely depresses me.

Dusk is closing in, making my way home less certain. I take the road back, instead of the fields. Felicity is spread below me, and on the far horizon, at the edge of the flood plain, I can see the lights of the city switching on—amber on the roadways, cool white in the buildings above.

Felicity seems remote and alien to me now, as does the city I have just come from. Suddenly, it's as if I belong nowhere, like Grandma Katherine. Whenever I think about making a life for myself, my mind returns to her.

8

I COME IN THE BACK WAY, stopping to knock the dirt off my sneakers before coming inside. Cookie, the dog, (Goldie's successor) is all over me, probably because she scents the St. Bernard.

I can't recall the house appearing so empty. I can hear Dad out on the front porch, fumbling through his pants pockets for the keys. Mom isn't home yet. She's left a note for us on the counter.

"I'll make a salad. Why don't you look down in the freezer for a couple of steaks?" Dad instructs me. I have the feeling this is his usual menu when he cooks for himself.

I don't think we've eaten alone together for years. "Is it often like this?" I ask. "I mean, is Mom tied up most evenings?"

"Not really," Dad says between mouthfuls. "Maybe once a week."

Silence, again. I used to think the silence between us was benign, now I'm not so sure. I envy Daniel his easy repartée with Dad. I know Dad has always loved me and always will, but I find myself wondering, does he like me? Not, do I belong? But, would I belong if we were not family? Which is a stupid question, because we are.

"I wondered," Dad says mid-swallow, "what you were up to when I got back. Running?" His face is screwed up as if he's trying to make sense of my outfit: a crew neck, holey sweats, and Dennis's electric blue socks.

"Just a long walk, up in the woods, past those new houses they're building."

"Those are something, aren't they?" Dad perks up like the Chamber of Commerce booster he is.

"How can anyone around here afford to live in them, though?"

"They say one of the new draft picks for the Buffalo Bills has bought one of those."

"Oh," I say lightly.

"I forgot, you're not interested in football anymore. Probably doesn't make any difference to you."

There is no point in protesting his appraisal. I've been judged. The verdict has been read. If you aren't interested in football around here, you must be an alien. For years Dad reminded me, "Even your mother gets into it."

He seems to have given up all hope for me. At the next big family gathering, he'll choose the moment to announce, portentously: "Laura doesn't care about football anymore."

Family members will bend forward and utter, "Really?" under their breaths. A few will exchange glances, as if Dad's admission only confirms what they've suspected about me all along, that I've always been too much of a smarty pants for them.

Dad puts down his fork and studies me with a concerned look sketched across his face. "You walked a long way. That leg of yours ever bother you since the accident?"

"Sometimes," I say. "In bad weather, it can ache. Or if I walk a long way." Aware of how I sound, I giggle. "I sound like an old lady!"

Dad laughs, too, relieved. The accident is still scary for both of us. I could have died. Grandma Katherine still blames Mom for what happened. A scar still runs across my forehead, as subtle as crazing on china. When I'm in the right light, it stands out. The light over the dinner table is just about perfect. Dad reaches over and presses my hand with one of his. If we were standing and not sitting, he might have hugged me. Thinking of the accident brings up an urge in him to hug me, to hold me close, as if, in retrospect, he wishes he could have protected me from the crash.

My father has always done his best to protect me from things. He proved sympathetic when I had misunderstandings or spats with Joanne and Melanie and, later, with boys. He once let me stay home all day from sixth grade because I was heartbroken over the loss of a boy I considered to be my boyfriend. I never saw my father so unspeakably angry as he was with his sister, my Aunt Bett, the time when she was babysitting and let us watch news footage of the Kennedy assassination. And there was the time Aunt Bett blurted out the news of their mother's death to Daniel and me as we sat on our front porch stairs. She told us more than the bare facts, indulging her own morbidity at our expense. She spoke of her mother's "terrible agony" and disclosed that her last words had been "unforgivable."

"You shouldn't have been so graphic. They're just children," he scolded his sister in the entranceway.

Daniel and I were in the living room with Mother, but we could still hear Dad arguing with Aunt Bett. I suppose he didn't want us to picture our grandmother in agony with her cancer, or to imagine that her last words weren't full of love or concern for the living. I suppose he just wanted to tell us gently, the way he had when his father died and he took us out in the canoe. But I wished he could believe I was strong enough to cope with whatever life would deal me.

Because old habits are hard to break, I wonder whether Dad isn't protecting me from something again. I give in to my curiosity. "I was wondering," I say, "with the economy and all, are you getting much new business?"

"I can't say that we are."

His eyes meet mine. I can see the fleck in his left eye, his "extra pupil." It's not a defect or anything, it's just something distinctive about him, something you'd notice.

"Of course," he adds, pushing his plate aside, "we hope to come out of it. It's a shame it has to be this way just as Daniel is starting out."

Dad walks across the kitchen with his dishes. He scrapes and rinses the plate before putting it into the dishwasher, something I never saw him do while I was growing up. "Just between you and me," he says, "it's worse than anyone suspects. I'm having trouble putting together the salaries. I think I may have to let Renee, our secretary, go. The three of us will have to manage with a word processor and an answering machine. It will be less complicated if Evan decides to retire."

Evan White is Dad's partner of long-standing, the one who hired Dad right out of architecture school. For the last ten years or so, my father has been the firm's acknowledged leader, while old Mr. White has gradually phased himself out of the business.

"Do you think he will?" I ask.

"The last two years have been pretty hard on him. I wouldn't be surprised."

"It must feel awful having to ask Mr. White to retire," I say.

"Well," Dad says, slapping down the dishcloth, "I've got a school board meeting. I'm sorry I can't stay. Maybe this will give you a chance to catch up on the sitcoms."

I smile indulgently at him. The fact that I don't own a television is something my family never fails to tease me about.

The garage door slams, reverberates, and I'm alone with the surprising knowledge Dad has left me. I'm strangely nostalgic. I want to go through the closet and the bureau drawers, maybe curl up with JFK retrospectives and clippings from man's first landing on the moon. My collection of old magazines and clippings doesn't document Vietnam, except maybe Mai Lai, and peters out too soon for Nixon's downfall. Those were the good years for the Brunner family, years before Dad got into the habit of pouring himself a stiff drink every night after work—and several refills—until he became weepy. He wasn't just worried about my injuries in the accident. I thought so at first, but his drinking continued after my recovery. I was puzzled by his behavior. Daniel was contemptuous and angry.

I remember one night, our family was playing a game of cards, and Dad, his usual moody self, had been refusing to cooperate. Finally, Daniel had had enough. He threw his cards down, and yelled, "Why are you being this way? Sometimes I think I hate you!"

I gasped, inwardly. That was the kind of remark for which I would never have even hoped for forgiveness.

Daniel managed to skip past it with his easy grace. But I will never forget my father's wounded face.

It wasn't until years later I learned that he and his firm were under investigation for bid-rigging city-commissioned building projects. As it turned out, his firm wasn't implicated, but Dad was required to testify. That put him in a precarious position in terms of lining up future commissions and dealing with suspicious contractors. The firm very nearly went out of business.

Looking back, I ache for Dad. When he kept things from us, I realize, it was not without a cost to himself.

LATER THIS SAME EVENING, I decide to visit Grandma Katherine. As I stroll down that shining waxed hallway at the nursing home, people stare at me through open doorways. Many are ready for bed, dressed in fuzzy bathrobes and furry slippers. It still seems wrong, improbable, that I could find a member of my family here.

But it is Grandma Katherine who throws open the door to greet me when I muster the courage to knock.

"Take off that big, heavy coat," my grandma coaxes.

I am reluctant to take it off, reluctant to make so firm a commitment to stay.

But Grandma Katherine already has her hand on my sleeve; she's not taking no as an answer. "So cold!" she exclaims, "it must be freezing outside!"

"The weather's changed," I say. "Haven't you been outside to feel it?"

She hasn't, and she expresses no interest in going out now. Not going outside! Is this a conscious, a willful, refusal on her part? Is she really giving up the world?

Grandma insists on fixing me a cup of cocoa, although all she's got now is a hot pot and those little packets. I make a mental note to bring along a box of the wafers she likes so much the next time I come.

"When will you be going back?" Grandma Katherine wants to know.

"I don't know," I tell her. "Soon."

Together, we go through catalogs of books on tape much as we had once poured over the Barron's directory of colleges. But then Grandma Katherine leans back with a sigh. "I'm tired of hearing about books," she says. And she won't tell me which ones I should order.

"When did you say you would be going back?" Grandma Katherine asks, again.

I avoid the question, and tell her instead: "I wish you could come and stay with me in my apartment. At least for a visit."

"Oh, I couldn't."

"Well, why not?" I press her. "I could meet you at the airport, and—"

"Maybe, back when I still had someone to travel with me, I could have," Grandma Katherine muses.

I sense that her word is final. It's like the time I tried to convince her to come to New York City with me for a long weekend after my sophomore year of college. I had been thinking back to when she and Grandpa had taken me to New York. We stayed at the St. Moritz overlooking Central Park, lunched at Schraft's, visited Broadway and the Met. It had been a great adventure. When I asked her to relive it with me, Grandma was obstinate. She chose to remember New York by its garbage strike and its pick-pockets. But that was Grandma, once she made up her mind.

"It's getting late, Grandma," I say. I've felt ill-at-ease the whole time I've been here. What has this place—with its institutional carpeting, its peach-colored bedspreads and draperies, its suites of honey oak furniture—got to do with Grandma Katherine and me? Seeing her surrounded by smiling, caring professionals, it's easy to get the feeling that Grandma Katherine is incompetent, and perhaps she is, although I resist thinking of her that way. With her free hand, she absently picks at the buttonholes of her cardigan as she walks with me to the lobby. Heads peer out again as we pass by. Although some of the gazes are vacant, not everyone here is blind. It's time for us to part, but Grandma hasn't let go of my arm. Maybe because she can no longer hold on to me with her eyes.

Back in the car, I'm too numb to cry. It would be easy to believe that there's nothing I can do for her. Too easy. I run my hand along the dashboard, feeling for the radio dial. Music, in place of all those words I didn't say. I could have told her that it saddened me to leave her here, that I was determined to make her a part of my life. Will I always hold myself apart, as I did with Melanie and Rob, with Joanne? Will it be the same for Dennis, for Grandma Katherine? I drive, feeling the vastness, the emptiness of the night. A few flurries drift down through the blackness, each one lingering briefly on the windshield before it disappears.

9

MY FATHER IS GONE by seven o'clock the next morning, before I'm even downstairs.

"Does Daniel ever take on some of these early-morning meetings?" I ask Mother over a cup of coffee. "It seems like project reviews would be just the right thing for someone who's new. You know, going over all that's involved, meeting with the clients."

"Sometimes," Mother says with a sigh. "But you know Daniel, he's no morning person." She pushes up from the table.

Mom has not asked me about my plans—immediate or eventual. Instead, she clunks her mug down into the dishwasher. "I guess you'll have the place to yourself today. I've got two luncheons in Franklin, then a bridal shower tea in Orchard Park. Don't ask me how I'll do it all."

She ducks her head into the freezer and takes inventory. "Six dozen lemon squares, six of the snow-on-the-mountain, three of the cheese wafers, two sponges, four dozen of the rolls, or make that breadsticks. My goodness, I'm getting low on some things. Good thing I've slated tomorrow for baking," she says, rearranging her hair and backing out the kitchen door.

I don't spend much time there, in the kitchen, staring out at the bare trees. There are productive uses for the way I'm feeling this morning. I could write a poem. I climb back up the stairs and riffle through my suitcase until I find what I'm looking for: a slightly crumpled manila folder with a sheaf of papers inside. I, too, take inventory. Here's my curriculum vitae, a few starts of poems, a chapter from my dissertation and, in case I feel inspired, a legal pad and a few sheets of bond.

With folder in hand, I head out for my car. I'll go in to Dad's office, borrow a typewriter, diddle a little with my résumé. Maybe visit the library. Or have lunch with Daniel. Browse the bookstores, the used record shops. A voice comes creeping into my consciousness, unnerving me with the question, *What are you good for?* Idle hands, I've been brought up to believe, are tools of the Devil.

The long drive following Route 5 along the lake summons memories of the summer I commuted in with Dad. He and I used to listen to the radio news and argue politics on the way. We followed the same sports. I learned how to change a tire and, because we drove a vintage '57 Chevy, how to wield the jumper cables, too. In short, we became buddies, and I believe he genuinely missed my company when September rolled around and it was time for me to go away to school. I know I missed his. I had fantasies about something happening to his business, so that I'd have to put college on hold and come back to help him, a sort of Girl Friday come to rescue him.

At nine forty-five, I arrive at the office. The secretary in the reception area is someone I don't know. Dad has been in and is already out again. Daniel hasn't been. Mr. White pokes his head out of his office and waves to me. The secretary, reassured that I am who I say I am, lets me proceed into Daniel's office, where I'll be out of the way.

I'm reading my curriculum vitae and wondering if I should order it differently, when Daniel comes in, all in a rush. He pulls out the lap drawer of his desk and shakes it until the Tylenol bottle rolls into sight. He throws his head back and gulps the pills down. Not for a moment do I assume that he is coming down with a cold. My guess? He's hung over.

"'Cuse me," he says, reeling out the door with his mug in search of water or coffee.

Seconds later, Daniel lands back in his chair. It's and executive model, expensive, leather and chrome. The air escapes its cushions. I had forgotten how big my brother is, how he makes every room seem too small for him. He has a loud voice, heavy footfalls, sweeping gestures. "Aaaah!" he says, after a deep swig of coffee. Perhaps catching a whiff of my disapproval, he adds, "Wait until you get into the grind, sister."

I smile. "Does ten a.m. qualify as the grind?"

He frowns, suddenly gruff and businesslike. "I get my work done. Look, I've gotten two new office projects this fall, both on my own. Now, I had to sell both companies on it, wine and dine them. But it was work, not play. Sanders Industries, here," he says as he sweeps his arm toward a drawing, "they're undergoing a complete retooling. They're redoing the plant, and I'm working on the office complex, the most efficient site arrangement, the grounds. They've still got the rail tracks, the canal and all that, and they still use 'em. But they want to use the best materials, the best design, go for a post-Industrial Revolution look, instead of chain link fences and smokestacks."

As he talks, with his adrenaline flowing and an intensity burning in his eyes, I can't help but admire him. He's the same boy who made Mother drive slowly over the Father Baker Bridge so he could look down on all the industry—the network of rail arteries and the ships on their way out from the harbor.

The phone rings. Daniel motions for me to wait. I have nothing better to do. I spread my papers out across my lap to appear more productive. Re-reading the story of my adult life from my scattered papers, I'm afraid my tombstone will read: *Paralyzed by Doubts*.

Maybe it's being female that drives me to be so cautious, so deliberate, so filled with doubt. After all, men just seem to *know*—or they pretend they do. Listen to Daniel. Don't try to tell my brother there are no absolutes.

But his confidence looks to be draining from him moment by moment as he stands talking on the phone. "Aw, come on, Irv, it can't be that bad. I'm sorry I didn't make it over on Friday, but I can come out today. Uh huh. Look, Irv, I'll be out to take a look. I'll talk to them. I'll redraw it if necessary. . . . Now? I'm real tied up. How's two this afternoon? . . . Yeah, yeah. . . . I know, I said I'm real sorry."

Irv must be chewing Daniel out—and Daniel must deserve it. He has to listen for another few minutes before he's allowed to hang up.

"Taking the heat," he says to me, and shakes his head. "I miss one appointment and he's all hepped up."

"Who was that?" I ask.

"Irving Klepman. Heard of him?"

"Sure, he's done a lot a projects with Dad over the years. It doesn't seem fair for him to be all over you for missing one appointment, if there aren't any other problems."

"Yeah, well, there are," Daniel admits. "And he's blowing his top. Of course, he's blowing the thing all out of proportion. Says he wants to turn it over to Dad, but I told him to hold on and give me another chance."

"And that's when you miss the appointment? Oh, Dan."

"What can I do now?" Daniel says, stretching in his executive chair. "Look, I was hoping we could have lunch in a couple of hours, but it looks like I'm swamped. What were you after, a typewriter? Why don't you go into Dad's office? After his meeting, I think he's going right on to a Chamber of Commerce luncheon."

Daniel walks with me to that familiar place. The light still filters in the way I remembered, and the photos depict our family fifteen years ago. Everything here looks just the same, except the room isn't overwhelmed by rolled blueprints and mach-ups with tiny trees, as Dad's office would have been in former days.

Daniel turns to leave me.

"Daniel?" I say.

He stops, mid-stride, as if he could read the gravity of the question I had been about to ask him.

I've never seen him look so vulnerable. "Oh, never mind," I say.

OF ALL THE MEMORIES I'VE KEPT OF DANIEL, the one that seems to me most true is Daniel during summer baseball season. He almost always captained a team. I remember watching those games through the long summer dusks, hearing the sound of the coach's voice calling out the names of Daniel's friends—Gary, Victor, Patrick, Kevin, Mark—his friends through all the grade school years, the

friends who are with my brother still. I remember the
coach strutting up and down the foul lines. The boys
complained bitterly about the way he drove them and
favored his own son. I can't think of a friend of Daniel's
who didn't come off the diamond crying at some point. I
admired them for the way they grimaced and smeared
their tears with their dirty forearms. They wanted so to
be tough.

My whole family always attended these games together. By the time Daniel was older, and in varsity baseball,
Grandma Katherine came, too. Dad carried in a mesh
folding chair for her. From time to time, I sat down cross-
legged next to her in the lush summer grass. But mostly,
I hung out behind the team bench, chasing after stray
balls, swinging a bat if I could get away with it. The high
school coach, Mr. Delvecchio, affectionately dubbed me
"the water boy," and ruffled my pixie-cut hair whenever
he passed by.

In all they stood up to, Daniel was the leader of these
boys. He orchestrated the team's banter when the other
team came to bat. His was the first palm slapped when a
runner crossed homeplate. He made quite a sight in his
catcher's getup, sending signals, hooting the other team's
players down when it came to that. He was absolutely
confident, or so it had seemed to me.

So who is that man with rolled shirt-sleeves, walking
out of my Dad's office? His confidence is no longer
absolute. He is pursued by doubt and is beginning to
sense it at his heels.

I'm concerned that, these days, Daniel looks forward
more to the victory celebrations in the bar than to playing the men's league games. I haven't seen Daniel's
friends for years now. I strain to picture them now—as

men—playing with the same spirit they had as boys. As if nothing has changed.

I lost my friends before I'd even graduated high school. But Daniel sees many of his buddies on weekly basis. By now, most of them have married, and some have kids. My brother is a late bloomer, in that respect. Even I am getting to be.

I ease into Dad's leather chair and heave a sigh. The business at hand is converting my academic-sounding curriculum vitae into the résumé of someone who is looking for a job. I decide to put education at the top, because my work experience looks so paltry. I'm hoping I can fill out the page.

By late afternoon, after having finished my photocopying and other errands, I meet Dad back at his office. He accepts a ride home with me, although it means he will have to catch one back with Daniel in the morning. Dad tops his head with the same hat he's worn for years—only it couldn't be the same one exactly, it must be a replacement—and waves goodbye to each person he greeted when he arrived in the morning, only in reverse order: the lawyers down the hall, the elevator operator, the garage attendant. The hat, so obviously out of style, like the rituals of greeting and leave-taking he maintains, strikes me as old-fashioned, even slightly ridiculous. I am aware that my father is becoming an old man.

"Heard you stopped in to see your grandmother last night. How was she?" Dad asks.

"I don't know, she seemed . . . different. Like, she hadn't been outside all day. And she wasn't as interested in her usual things."

"Well, I guess she's still getting adjusted. And it wasn't that nice yesterday. I can't say I blame her for staying inside."

"Do you think she could be mad at us, and the way she's acting could have to do with that?" I ask and hear a subtle accusation creep into my voice.

"I don't have any idea, Laurie." Dad frowns, trying to imagine. "Except that doesn't sound like your grandmother. We can ask your mother. She was planning to stop by and see how Grandma was doing on her way back this afternoon."

"Sounds like a busy day," I say. "She had a couple things to cater first."

"That's the way her business has been going lately." He shrugs. "She may not have told you, but she's had to hire more help. She's got two part-time employees now."

"Really? Mom, with employees? Who are they?"

"Renata Schmitt, who used to work at the drug store, and somebody you don't know, Karla Mueller. She's got kids just going into high school, and she only puts in a few hours a week, to help your Mom out in a pinch."

As we pull into the driveway, I spot another car I don't recognize.

It's Daniel," Dad tells me. "He's brought his fiancée, Susan, over so you can meet her. Did your mother and I forget to mention they'd be coming?"

"No, I think maybe you did and I've just forgotten." I comb my fingers through my hair. I've been so preoccupied with my grandmother, and thinking about the past, that I've let the present go out of focus.

In the past, I looked forward to sitting at the top of the stairs during my parents' parties, watching the grownups as they shuttled back and forth between the living room, the dining room, and the bar set up in the kitchen. Perched above it all, I was a budding social critic, observing with great disdain and amusement all the goings-on in which the grownups revealed themselves to be as silly as I had always suspected. Of course, they had too much to drink and talked in loud, absurd voices. They told bawdy jokes and played a game that involved passing oranges from person to person without using their hands. And, because even my parents' generation was affected by the Sexual Revolution, there were clandestine exchanges made below me in the hall. Affairs were begun and flourished, and sometimes came to messy endings. Rumors spread that a wronged wife Krazy-glued the penis of her sleeping husband to his stomach. Word of this travelled quickly back to town from the county hospital emergency room. All the adults knew who the unfortunate man was, but they wouldn't say his name out loud.

Now that my parents are in their fifties, the pace of their parties has slowed. They're more likely to host family gatherings. I'm no longer able to escape to the stairwell where I can watch them from afar. So I bear up, smile, and receive the hand of Daniel's fiancée Susan, who, I can see from her blonde hair, polished teeth, and her string of pearls is a real thoroughbred. This one has the works.

"Hey, Sis." Daniel slaps me on the shoulder, then ducks around me into the kitchen for a beer.

During dinner, the topic for conversation is the stroganoff recipe. Although it is a trade secret of Mom's catering business, and I know she won't give it away, Susan persists in a half-hearted attempt to obtain it. Such persistence passes for flattery in Felicity. After dinner,

Daniel and Susan describe in minute detail the house they would like to buy. It's up on Sandstone Road—in fact, just two houses past the Martin's. Susan says it's "not inexpensive," but considering its age, a good buy.

Mother clears her throat. Her face shows a certain strain. "Not to pry into your finances," she says, "but do you know how much those houses are going for? And, because of their age, there's not a one that isn't going need a lot of work."

"Those houses up on Sandstone will be going up in value, not down," Susan counters sweetly but with an edge in her voice.

Daniel leans forward, reaches for his beer. (It's none of my business, but I count his empties—one at the table, two by the sink.) "I agree. Those houses are way under-valued," he says.

"Well, that's your business, if you think you can swing it. But your mother was trying to tell you that she and I have some experience here you might want to take advantage of," Dad says. "No pressure, we could just roll over the numbers together, get a feel for whether this house might be feasible for you. And I can't cosign for you like I did with your first car, but I can get you an appointment with the right person down at the bank."

My mother flashes Dad a look. "We can talk more about it later."

The conversation moves on to wedding plans. I'm supposed to go in for a fitting. I try and imagine the torture: Mother and Susan fully dressed while I'm standing in my underwear, having my measurements read aloud by a lady with straight pins in her mouth. And paying for the ugly gown, that will be torture, too. Maybe Mother will help me so my check doesn't bounce. My finances are

abysmal at the moment because I bought myself a citrus
tree and thirty-dollars' worth of books to cheer myself
when Dennis and I split up. I have to maintain my car—
even if just barely—but beyond texts and fees, food and
the rent for my apartment, I have no expenses. I don't live
extravagantly.

Daniel finally does get around to asking about
Grandma Katherine.

"Where is she staying?" Susan asks.

"The Evergreens," Dan tells her.

"What a preposterous name for a nursing home," I say.
"As if a metaphor will be enough to keep those people
from crumpling up and dying."

"English majors!" Daniel snorts. "You're easy to pick
out in a crowd."

Mom's hand covers her smile. "Anyway, Laura, there
are evergreens. Literal ones. It's not just a figure of
speech."

"Where is it?" Susan asks.

"On Park Street, in Franklin, not too far from where
you went to school." He address me. "Did you know
Susan was a Sacred Heart girl?"

I hadn't even met Susan until two hours ago. "Oh, really?" I am able to muster in reply.

Susan doesn't seem to contradict what little I know
about Sacred Heart Academy, the private high school
where prosperous Roman Catholic families send their
daughters—daughters who will later become nurses,
teachers, and ultimately wives. That a few of them go on
to other things is only incidental, not a result of the ideals
the sisters have held up for aspiration.

When I change the subject back and ask Mom how Grandma Katherine was this afternoon, I find Mom was running behind schedule and didn't have time to stop.

"I thought not having the responsibility for Grandma Katherine would give me a lot more time," Mom says. "Somehow, that's not the case."

"You're not as stressed out," Daniel observes, and I'm surprised to realize he's right. Mom does seem happier, lighter now that Grandma Katherine is gone, even if I have caught her more than once gazing up wistfully from the second floor landing at those stairs that used to lead to Grandma Katherine's apartment.

No one comments on how odd it feels to be eating a family dinner without Grandma. The family has made a trade-off I'm going to have to get used to. Grandma Katherine's chair is occupied by someone I hardly know who is about to become my sister-in-law. I'm hoping Dan and Susan plan to stop by The Evergreens on their way home.

Susan follows me out into the kitchen to help me with the dishes, on the pretext, I suppose, of trying to get to know me better. "Where's Dan? Disappeared when it's time to help? Some things never change," I say, sounding like a sister talking.

Susan just smiles and shrugs. As she collects the dishes and I load the dishwasher, we do our best to exchange a few facts. She's a physical therapist and enthusiastic about her hobbies, which are skiing, antiques, and Junior League. She doesn't take much interest in what little I say in description of my work at graduate school. She'd know me better if she were to meet me at my study carrel and we were to walk together back to my apartment for lunch. But the same could be said about anyone in my family.

Just then, Daniel barges into the kitchen. He points at his watch. "Look, it's seven forty-five, and I said I'd meet Gary at eight."

"You're going out tonight? I thought you were coming over to my house," Susan says.

"I know, I forgot to mention it to you, but Mark is back in town, and we all wanted to take him out."

"Mark!" I exclaim. "What's he up to?"

"He's out of medical school, finishing up his residency in Minnesota. Oh, and he's married."

"But we were going to work out the guest list!" Susan reminds him.

"Don't hassle me about it. We'll get to the guest list, don't worry."

Daniel as a married man—that's going to be an interesting development. I look across at Susan, with sympathy. Will Daniel become the sort of man who goes out to tie one on, leaving behind his passive-aggressive wife? It is clear to me what Dan sees in Susan. She'll know which way to get her hair coiffed, which clubs to join, which furniture brand is best for impressing the firm's clientele. Dan will join a softball team; Susan will have her luncheons with the Junior League. Their future together sounds terrible to me, but then I never understood these things.

As I stack the last few fragile pieces of glassware in the dish drainer, Mom reappears with a dishcloth in hand.

"That's okay, Mom, I was just going to let them drain."

"I don't mind," Mom says, which is my signal to pick up a dish towel and join her.

This ritual, in which the women analyze the subtext of family dinners over the dishes, goes back years, and the two of us have been central characters as long as I can remember. We've often been joined by Aunt Bett or Uncle Kurt's wife, Marianne. Those who didn't join us were in especial danger of being discussed, like Cousin Karl's wife who still remained childless after eight years of marriage and always dressed in business suits; or Bett's daughter, Elizabeth (in Aunt Bett's absence), who was just a little "hard to take"; or Great-aunt Paula who, long after her recovery from yet another surgery, maintained her reputation as long-suffering, although she had mostly outlived her contemporaries by a decade. (A family wag, unafraid to air the nearly universal view that Paula was merely a hypochondriac, once wickedly challenged us to imagine what Paula looked like naked, scars and all.)

The current of this family gossip rode us over whole decades, with characters and plot veering little from their expected course. I usually liked these sessions, except when I was made witness to Mother's belittling of Grandma Katherine. I felt disloyal for listening, and smiling or laughing would have made me complicitous. But mostly, the communal will around the kitchen sink matched my own, and I liked the sense of smugness that came from belonging.

Now, standing here alone with Mom, I feel awkward, unsure of what to say. But Mom fills in for me, muttering: "I wonder how they think they'll pay for it."

I realize, with a shock, that she's still annoyed by Daniel and Susan and their profligate spending. Or perhaps it's their disregard for her counsel that bothers her. I don't say anything, knowing that later, if things fall back again into the old order—Daniel is above reproach—my trespass won't be taken kindly.

Mom asks, "What did you think of Susan?"

"I don't know her well enough to feel comfortable around her yet, but I got the sense she and Dan belong together," I say, relieved not to have said what was running through my mind: *They deserve each other.* I find myself wondering what the aunts would have to say.

Mom tells me she's exhausted, but she's going out to see Grandma Katherine. I'm pleased. Dan and Susan should have gone, but that, too, is best left unsaid.

"What do you think of the nursing home?" Mom asks, wiping the water spots out of the sink.

"It looks better than I expected, for that kind of place," I say, rearranging the antique salad cruets in their stand and carrying them back out to the dining room.

As I rejoin Mother in the kitchen, I'm struck by how tired she looks. "It must have been difficult living with her these past months, more difficult than I could imagine," I say to break the silence.

Mom puts lotion on her hands. "She always perks up when she's around you." She pauses. "You don't see her the same way we do."

"I guess it must be a relief not always having to worry about her."

"What other choice did we have?" Mom asks defensively. She finishes drying the milkglass butter dish, then lays her towel aside. "There are some things I wish I could take back," she nearly whispers. "I regret we didn't have a better relationship, or more of a relationship."

I look at my mother with surprise. "You aren't angry with her?"

Mother's face isn't set in that hard expression I remember from adolescence. Instead, she looks vulnerable, sad. She presses her lips together, shakes her head. "She seems so helpless. I just feel sorry for her."

CLOSE TO TEN O'CLOCK, Dennis calls. I lie back on my parents' bed, the way I did through confidential phone calls in my adolescence. When I stretch my legs up, I can see them reflected across in the mirror. Rising to my knees, I take in my entire reflection. I am coming to an age, when youthful promise either gets fulfilled or it is broken. Have I broken my promise? I scrutinize my reflection, but nothing in my straight-faced mien gives me a clue.

"I'm worried about you," Dennis says.

Of course he is. But why didn't he worry more about me all those nights I struggled alone through papers I had no desire to write? Why didn't he worry the day I wept in the hall outside the office of my graduate advisor? The fact is, her comments were so withering I have never told anyone *all* of what she said. So, to be fair, Dennis could not have known. My advisor questioned my motives. She questioned the relationship I had with Dennis in connection with my work. I realize now one has nothing to do with the other, but I didn't then, and my tears were tears of anger, of defeat.

But I try to do as Dennis counsels and think back to why I chose graduate school in the first place. Was it because of my grandparents, rather than because of me? I'm not sure the persona I took on then was mine. Even so, I was glad for the long hours of reading and the runs I took along the lakefront after swallowing books whole.

Still, it didn't take long before I became disenchanted with my program of studies. To absorb what I read, that was one thing, but to write about it beyond my own reaction? I had never done *that* before. I found myself stretching for analogies. Interpretation was something I imposed, not something organic coming out of the body of the text. And from there, my troubles in graduate school blossomed.

It was at about that time I first met Dennis. And perhaps without the distraction he provided, I would have focused more on my disappointment with my studies. Perhaps my unhappiness could even have caused me to leave the program. But I doubt it. I took comfort in books, although more often in books of my own choosing.

Dennis sat with me in Medieval seminar most of the semester before we noticed each other. One day, late in November, I had been out running, and spotted a person in the water. A swimmer was calmly lapping the length between breakwalls. I recognized Dennis as he emerged, and called out to him. For a moment, we both stood silent, panting and staring at each other. His chest was heaving after the exertion of his swim. We talked—a funny, disjointed conversation. "Hey," he finally said. "That's my towel behind you. Would you mind tossing it over?"

"Of course," I said. "I'm sorry, you must have been freezing."

But I was impressed that what he must have been was brave.

I STAND AND STRETCH with the phone pressed to my ear.

Dennis is saying, "That's I wanted to tell you about. I've had a breakthrough on my dissertation this week. I'm through about four chapters, you know, and starting on my fifth, but what never occurred to me is—"

"Dennis," I interrupt. "I hope you can appreciate the sincerity in what I'm about to say. In the first place, I thought we were through seeing each other, and I don't see what good it's doing to keep phoning each other over every last thing as if our relationship had never ended."

"Nobody asked me if I wanted it to end."

"In the second place, even if I did want to talk with you, the last topic, the absolute last topic of conversation I'd choose would be that of your dissertation. In case you've forgotten, my dissertation topic has been rejected three times! And here you are just sailing through yours. Not that I'm not glad for you. I just wish I could bring myself to write on an academically-approved topic. But I can't."

"Look," Dennis says in his reasonable tone of voice, "I'm bringing it up because I thought it might interest you. What I'm finding, as I look through all the Hughes and Plath sources, is that their relationship was cross-pollinating, far more than I had guessed."

"And you find that surprising?"

"It's true, I suppose, I figured their relationship to be of minor importance to his work. That's why I hadn't given it much attention. So go ahead and accuse me of being an ignoramus, if that's what you're thinking. At least I'm going to be honest about what I've found. And believe me, that's going to mean scrapping a lot of what I've already done."

"You mean, you'll be going back?"

"And rewriting it, yes. I might have a tough time with my advisor, so I'm going to really work up my arguments before going in to him."

"I have to give you credit, Dennis. I'm envious. I'd like to have a crack at that topic myself."

"Do you want to? I could find something else to write on."

"After all the work you've done? Don't be ridiculous!"

"But I wouldn't have looked at it the way I did—I wouldn't have *seen* the topic—if you hadn't taught me to look that way."

"Dennis, you're the one who went through the process. The topic is yours. I appreciate what you're trying to do for me, but let's make this the end of the discussion."

I hold the phone away from my ear for a moment, listening as a door opens downstairs and footsteps enter. Below my feet, on the rug, the dog tenses. But it's just Dad, and we both relax again.

"Are you still there?" Dennis asks.

"I'm here."

"Don't you see the irony of it? I'll probably be awarded a women's studies position somewhere. And what about you?"

"I don't know. Maybe it's no use. Maybe I just can't think their way."

"Maybe someone with an original mind is what they need most." Dennis offers me a way back and a challenge. I think I would hug him if I could.

The stairs creak under the cushion of carpet as Dad moves up them. He casts his shadow over the lamp's halo and reaches to tap me on the shoulder.

"Excuse me," I say to Dennis, and turn to Dad.

"I'm sorry, Laura," he says, and his voice is straight-edged, sober. "I'm going to have to interrupt. I've got a phone call I have to make before it's too late."

I tell Dennis goodbye and go out of the room without closing the door. I feel like sitting down and poking through the pocket change and matchbooks in the lap drawer of my father's desk. If there were any secrets to be revealed about him, I would find them there—or at his workbench in the cellar, where he spends his private moments, has his private thoughts.

"See you downstairs?" I ask him from the hall.

"Yeah, I suppose I'll be back down."

I'm standing in the hall bathroom with the door open, brushing out my hair. I'm not really paying attention, but I hear Dad say Evan's name on the phone. I know what he's doing. Poor Dad. He's put off letting Evan go for as long as he thinks he can.

I pour myself a ginger ale and take it down into the basement, then stand quietly and sip it under the buzz of the old fluorescent lights. Paint flecks the marred old bench where Dad and I have worked side-by-side on many a project. Upstairs, at this moment, I know Dad feels he is betraying his honor by asking Evan to step down, or, as the euphemism goes, take an early retirement. Dad and I share precious few traits in common. But one of them is a strong sense of personal honor. Another is loyalty.

"Laura, is that you?" Dad calls down the basement stairs. He must have seen the door ajar.

"Yes, Dad," I answer, even though I dread seeing his face, ashen as it must be after making that call.

He comes down two stairs, peers at me. He doesn't look so bad, though, just tired. "I think I'll pour myself something, too," he says. "Wait for me."

Later, leaning back against the bench, he says, "Well, that's that. Evan's a good fellow. He didn't take it too badly."

"I'm sorry," I say, because for all his years of dedication, I know it's bitter fruit for him to reap.

Dad bites down on his upper lip. "That's life," he says. "There wasn't a thing I could have done to change it."

He turns away from me and starts reshelving tiny jars of nuts and screws, and I know our conversation is over.

10

THE ROLLING PIN CLATTERS as my mother pushes it over pale dough. Her forearms do all the work. She doesn't use the weight of her body or the strength that comes down from her shoulders. Mom is not the sort of person who thinks of herself as having strength.

She casts a sharp eye on me when I enter the kitchen in my bathrobe. I sense she has been at work for some time. A buzzer sounds, and she pulls two sheets of snow-on-the-mountain from the oven. Several pans of lemon bars go in to replace them. I scour around for the coffeepot and find it draining upside down next to the sink. I quietly go about making a pot for myself.

"Your father told me that Dennis called again last night," Mother says.

"Yes, that's right."

"Well, is that back on again? He certainly seems anxious to stay in touch."

I duck around Mom to see if I can rummage through and find something in the bread box. Two hot dog rolls, a stale heel of bread, then, finally, pay dirt: half a package of English muffins. "Oh," I venture, slicing a muffin apart, "he's just worried about me missing classes. And he wanted to talk about dissertation topics."

The deafening blare of the food processor cuts into the second half of my sentence. "What are you making now?" I shout, and notice my voice is too loud by the end of the question.

"About five things at once." Mother smiles. "But you're changing the subject. Your father and I are concerned, too, about your missing a whole week of classes we've paid for—and the money isn't easy to come by. Your father has had to talk to Evan about early retirement."

"I *know*, Mother."

She looks startled. "You do? Well, it was a very difficult thing for your father to do." Taking a few steps over to the refrigerator, she begins to rummage through.

I pull my muffin from the toaster, burning my fingertips.

Mom hands me a jar. "Here, use this blueberry jam and you won't need to use butter. I notice you've been keeping yourself nice and trim lately."

I spread on some of the jam and sniff the jar. I guess it won't hurt me. "Missing a week of classes won't set me too far behind. I'll look at someone else's notes. Besides, I needed the time away. I needed perspective. Now I think I know how I'm going to approach this dissertation."

"Oh?" My mother lifts her eyebrows and intones patiently, as if she hasn't asked this question a dozen times before, "And what will your subject be?"

"Well, I still have the rest of this year to really nail it down. I know I'm not going to do Virginia Woolf or anyone like that. She's been done *ad nauseum*. And I'd like to do a woman, but I can't do anyone too modern. That's frowned upon. Too bad. There are a few men in my period with whom I really feel a bond. That would be the easiest, to go ahead and do one of them. Or I could write on

one of the minor women poets, and maybe that would
lead me to something less conventional—a biography, for
instance, that would encompass a critical look at her
poetry. But the one article I've ever gotten published was
on the diaries of homesteading women, and I think I'm
going to go with that."

"Well, good," says Mother. "If it's been published as an
article already, I expect your advisor will be more receptive to it."

"And just to make sure, I'm switching advisors. That's
another decision I've come to."

Mother looks up from her kneading, but says nothing.

"Mind if I turn the radio on?" I say. "I haven't heard
the news yet, and I'm not used to only having the afternoon paper." I walk the few steps over to the radio. When
I switch it on, the broadcaster announces the Nobel Prize
in literature was awarded to Gabriel García Marquéz. I
clap my hands. "Oh, listen! The Nobel Prize! I wonder
what Dennis will think of García Marquéz winning it."

Hearing the Nobel Prizes announced each year, on a
string of cool October mornings, marks time passing for
me. I'm also made aware that now I am an adult and
expected to be productive. Usually Dennis or I—whichev-
er of us first hears the news—gets in touch with the other,
so we can commiserate over it. "But I could hardly call
him now," I say, mostly to myself.

"Go ahead, if you'd like," Mom says.

"No, he'd be at class." I sigh and gulp the rest of my
coffee. I'm reluctant to get up. I feel surprisingly comfortable here with my mother.

It's as if, in removing Grandma Katherine, we have
removed an obstacle from between us. Mother and I had
once been companions, but that was years ago, back

when I was in grade school, and my memory of that time is hazy. I remember she had read long fairy tales aloud to me and stroked my hair as I pretended sleep. We hiked together in the woods. She taught me how to bake cookies and cakes—as well as cooking lessons that never sank in, like how to roll a pie crust.

I CLIMB UPSTAIRS AND DRESS in one of Dennis's sweatshirts again. I am determined to pick some of the apples in the orchard behind the house. Mother tries to discourage me; she says the apples are old and no good anymore. But the thought of the fruit just withering on the stem, the starlings circling down to pick at it, bothers me, so I march out anyway with a box in hand.

My mom was right, the fruit is blemished. But last night's frost was not prolonged enough to turn the flesh mushy. If I pick enough, I can press some cider. I wear Dad's barbeque apron with the deep pocket so I won't have to keep climbing back down to the box. I'm reminded of how, in years past, everybody helped pick. I miss the company today.

The orchard has always been a place I've come to let the weight of my worries lift from me. I can go back in time to those days when Daniel and I were children. Back to the neighborhood softball games, which Joanne and I would heckle and interrupt until finally the boys realized it would be easier just to let us play. The orchard served as the far outfield then, and that's where Joanne and I were assigned. Sometimes, we would liven up the game by drubbing the infield with apples, but that was a desperate ploy. It often resulted in being thrown out of the game. She and I played football with Daniel and his friends, too, in the field adjacent to the orchard. The games often degenerated from touch to tackle. I can remember once laying near the edge of the field with my wind knocked out, gaping at the unbroken sky above me and wondering if I was about to be levitated straight up into heaven.

As a child, I would look off in the direction of our house, and beyond, out over the flood plains, and imagine the curvature of the earth. Beyond our house, I could watch for sunsets, or approaching storms.

After a while, Mom comes out to join me. I tell her I was remembering the games Dan and I used to play and how we used to argue out here in the orchard when we were commanded, as we inevitably were, to do a tree together.

"Not all the time, but a bit," Mother acknowledges.

"I remember that we always ended up pelting each other with rotten apples. There was nothing worse than a bull's eye with one of those!"

"One of these?" Mother finds one on the ground, and she turns it in her hand. She smiles up at me mischievously.

"Mom!" I scream, so that she smiles sweetly and drops the brownish-skinned apple.

For a few minutes, we pick in silence. She chooses the fruit cautiously and never pulls an apple she will later discard. I have always admired her discerning eye.

I confess to her, "You know, I'm a little worried about Dan, and I wanted to talk with you about it."

Her face clouds over, and I expect her to accuse me of being unnecessarily critical. Daniel is a risky subject to bring up to my mother. But she says, "What about Daniel?"

"Well, have you noticed how much he seems to be drinking?"

Mother nods. "Of course, after all those years I struggled with your father when his drinking got heavy."

"Have you said anything to him?"

"I've made remarks. But I can't restrict what he does anymore. It's his life."

"Don't you think a really serious talk would make him stop and consider?"

"Only if it came from his father. He wouldn't listen to me." Mother stoops to empty the apron I've handed down to her, then turns her face up to me again. "Our relationship isn't the same as it used to be. It started to change sometime when he was back in high school, and even now, he's still very much his father's son."

An apple slips loose from my grip. "Oops, sorry," I say. "But Dad wouldn't think his drinking was a problem."

"Exactly," Mom says sadly.

Late in the afternoon, after taking a long break and writing some notes to myself about my ideas for the dissertation, I climb back up into one of the orchard trees. I'm slowing down. I've picked several boxes full. There will be plenty to make a cider pressing. I climbed the tree again because I like it so well up here, surrounded by the soft rustle of leaves, the tangy perfume of the apples.

The comfortless slate sky has lifted. Balmier winds blow in a blue sky and high broken clouds. The peaceful, observant state I'm in now is the same state I achieved here so often in adolescence. There isn't a thing happening within miles that could escape my notice. I hear gravel crunch on the driveway below. Mom is in the house. I resist the impulse to jump down and see who has come to

visit. I'm not ready, yet, to give up my quiet sense of sus-
pension.

I think of Dennis's blue-black eyes. Like Grandpa and
Grandma Katherine, Dennis and I have our own love
story.

One bright Sunday afternoon, Dennis and I took a sail-
boat out with his friend Alex and became part of the
informal regatta we had watched with longing from our
windows. All that past week, we had been trapped behind
our study tables, immobilized by finals. So on Sunday, I
felt strangely light and free as I sunned myself beneath
white sails. I felt content to be carried along only by the
whims of wind and water. Dennis brought a book along,
which annoyed me. But Alex was completely at ease. He
stretched himself languorously on the deck and let the
breezes stir his gold-blond forelock. Something about
him suggested irreverence. He seemed almost to scoff
when he glanced across at me. And, whenever he looked,
his scrutiny was too well-formed, too prolonged.

At first, I responded by lowering my eyes. Every year
since I had gone off to college, I had shed a few pounds,
and I felt attractive and out-of-place in my bikini. Out of
wonderment, I touched my hand to the taut drum of skin
which stretched between my ribs, and was surprised
when Alex reached over to touch me, too. He rubbed me
playfully on the belly with his tanned hand.

I was unaccustomed to the sensation of sexual power,
which felt something like steering a sports car down a
steep series of curves. Dennis had put aside his book by
then, and kept mooning across at me. Whenever Alex
turned away to make some sort of nautical adjustment,
Dennis closed in, grasping my hand and whispering to me
with an urgent but confidential tone in his voice. It

seemed the same stimuli of brightness and motion that had brought on a lightness in me gave him a sense of the elemental, the important. He hoped to have an effect on me; his dark face strained with the effort of expression. I have to admit he looked beautiful that way, with his eyes so earnest and intense, and his otherwise taut lips distended with a question. But I didn't want to be reminded, just then, of the seriousness of my own nature.

By mid-afternoon, the sky had clouded over, and Dennis wanted to head back to shore. Alex and I broke out fresh beers, determined not to give up the day. Dennis was beginning to brood over upcoming finals, but I knew I had studied enough. I needed to relax and let the knowledge settle. So Alex and I kept up an easy banter while Dennis stared out across the water, looking back from time to time at me.

It was strange the way he looked at Alex and me, because it seemed to show approval. He appeared to take pleasure in watching us flirt. I had seen him do this before. I remembered dancing passionate, fast numbers with one of his friends while he sat looking on. Perhaps it was vicarious participation on his part that made his eyes so full of luster.

I slipped my shirt on over my head, for the wind had turned suddenly colder. Working with Alex, I secured the main sheet and helped to steer with the tiller. There was more to do, now that the breeze had stiffened, and I enjoyed the undercurrent of excitement between us, the way our bodies accidently brushed together.

The lake had gone choppy and, definitive as the edge of a blind, a sheet of black clouds was advancing outward from the horizon. As the boat heeled, barely skimming above the water, the cold wind and spray broke against our backs.

Dennis and I exchanged looks of uneasy acknowledgment. We had drifted out too far from land, lured by gentle water and an easy breeze. And now, the boat rode on a knife's edge. The lake churned, and gusts of wind slicked our shirts to our backs. Even Alex had lost his smirking confidence.

A sudden down draft drove the bow violently into the whitecaps. I focused on Dennis. I was aware of the connection between us. I felt the impact before I hit the water. It was a lift, a hesitation. Then a cold, dark force sucked me under. It held me there as I flailed in the agitated foam. Finally, it released me. When I surfaced, I felt shaken, alienated from myself. It took me a moment to remember how to breathe. I felt myself alone, part of the sky and water.

Nearby, I could hear a small sound, remote from me. Its pitch was different from that of the waves breaking around me. I was able to concentrate on it. Despite the heavy swells and the icy paralysis of my limbs, I tried to move in the direction of the sound.

Then I heard Dennis call for me. "Laura?"

Never had a voice sounded so lovely, or so far away.

"Laura?" he called again.

Had Laura been my name? The sound of his voice made me long for something. Still, I could not separate myself from the water.

Not once during that time did I look at my body. It didn't seem a part of me. So it was a shock to see a human hand cut through a wave. An arm emerged after it, and then a body. A head with dark hair lifted once. A mouth opened to gulp in air. Dennis gasped on water when he saw me. "Laura!" he said.

"Yes, yes!" I looked into the depth of his eyes, and felt sorry for having skimmed over them before.

Kicking violently, he held me for a moment in the water, and I felt the infusion of warmth. His shoulders convulsed, white against the black of the water, and he allowed himself a few deep sobs. It seemed foolish, in the midst of all that water, but we were both crying. He caught himself and held me in a tearless, lucid gaze.

We turned from each other and started swimming. I could see Alex far ahead, riding out the waves in the shell of his boat. Was it a kind of grace that made him appear untouched by the swirling water that surrounded him?

As I fought my way through the raging lake, Dennis was at my side. I glimpsed one of his arms, mid-stroke, in the instant before it disappeared beneath the water. I saw that it was all sinew and knew that nothing ever came easily for Dennis. If only he had lifted his head, he would have seen the look of pure admiration I gave him. But he missed it. And there would be no way for me to repeat it, to offer it later as a gift.

THE SUN HAS DROPPED halfway to the horizon; light slants through the remaining leaves which flutter feebly in the breeze as if only held by thread. The heat is intense for this time of the year, and welcome. I'm sitting in my favorite apple tree, feeling almost drowsy. Two figures approach from the house. In this light it's difficult to identify them, but then one gestures—a cutting motion of the hand—and I know immediately it's Dennis. I slip down easily from the tree—it's a Jonathan, and its limbs are relatively smooth. I meet Dennis halfway between the orchard and the house, near my fifth-grade sugar maple. I might have stood apart from him. He pulls me close, even lifting me a little off the ground. My first look at him is blurred, too close to be in focus. His chest is warm, his grip firm around my waist. Our thighs and our hips press together. I had forgotten the feel of him.

He brushes some loose hair away from my face. Doesn't say anything. Just looks.

And what am I to say? Later on, perhaps, I can draw back, ask his purpose. But now, I walk around with him to the front of the house, arm-in-arm, glad of his presence.

We stop to look at the rental car which has just brought him five hundred miles. Dennis raps it lightly on the hood. "So this is Felicity."

I see him tilt his head back, see his eyes move over the uneven clapboards. I know he doesn't see the house as I do. He sees its flaws. He sees the places where the gloss has worn off the paint, where the surface has begun to craze.

"Where's the fire damage?" he asks.

"You'll have to walk around to the other side of the house," I reply, and lead him past the lilac thicket and the bed of ivy.

We both gape up at the hole. Plastic has been tacked over the opening, but dark streaks radiate out from its center, giving it the ominous appearance of a melanoma. Standing so near the damage leaves me with a tinge of smoke on my tongue. We turn and walk together back to the orchard. We walk an arm's length apart because we need to be careful and give one another space.

Whatever possessed you to come? I ought to ask him. But I don't because, truthfully, I'm happy he did.

Later, we hold hands at the supper table just as if I had invited him for a visit. Mom and Dad assume I'll be heading back to Chicago with Dennis, but they suggest we stay the weekend so they can get to know Dennis better.

"You won't be missing too much if you don't drive back until Monday, now will you?"

"No, Mr. Brunner, I don't have to teach until Tuesday."

"Call me Frank," my dad insists.

"Mind if we walk now?" I ask. "We'll pick up the dishes later."

"Go on," my father says, and he waves us away with a big, lavish wave meant to encourage us to have fun.

I look back at Dad who is standing in the kitchen. He hasn't changed much in appearance over the years. His waist has thickened, maybe, but his shoulders are straight and appear firm. Of course, he blesses us. He was young once, too.

Outside, there is light enough to walk by. "Let's go up to the woods," I suggest. "That's the best place."

I take Dennis on a slightly different route. We follow old, broad thoroughfares I tell him once were logging roads. I show him the collapsed bridge, point out the path I took up to Joanne's. The last daylight is filtering down through the trees, but I'm not concerned. Even in the dark, I can find my way back from here. We linger because we have so much to talk about.

"I don't know what you meant by going away. Either time," Dennis says.

"You know it's because of Grandma Katherine I came out here. What's troubling you is why I left you in the first place, and why once I got here I stayed."

"Are they related?"

"Might be. Let me talk about why I left you. That's something that's been coming clearer the longer I've stayed away."

"Sounds bad," Dennis says, trying to inject levity.

But I'm in no mood to back off from the subject at hand because, at this moment, I have as good a grasp of it as I've ever had, probably ever will.

"Now, listen," I say. "This is important. What happened is that I somehow couldn't separate you from the rest of what I was doing. I somehow couldn't separate your success from my failure."

Dennis puts both hands on my shoulders to stop my progress ahead of him on the path. He studies my face in the dim light. "Do you mean that you can now?"

I can only tell him the truth, but I turn away from his gaze. "I don't know. There's a chance, but really only time will tell. Who knows how this project will go? Sometimes I've thought that the wiser thing to do would be to part ways and hope we'd meet somewhere on the Midwest tenure track, Dr. Brunner and Dr. Andersen. Then we could fall in love all over again. And I'd feel free to."

"You don't really mean that."

"I do, if only it were so simple as just walking away. But it isn't."

He pulls me to him then, his hand pressing the nape of my neck.

"When we're together," I say, "I want to be thought of for my own sake. Not just in relation to what you're doing."

I do not describe the mental picture I have of Grandma Katherine that keeps flooding in, unbidden. Of course, she is only as I imagine her to have been, and I know the truth is rarely as simple as the one I visualize.

"I know," he murmurs, "your failure, my success. Don't let yourself think in those terms."

I lean my head against his shoulder and sigh. "It's hard, it's hard," I whisper, as we stand together among the immense trees.

In a sense, I realize, my advisor was right. She is a woman. Perhaps she had made some of the same mistakes I have. Still, she questioned my motives. She confirmed my self-doubt. She could have been more understanding.

Dennis holds me beneath the same tress that watched impassively while Joanne and I scrambled and played, scattering the mat of leaves, scuffing up the loam, hiding behind their scratchy trunks. Joanne is lost to me. I wouldn't know where to begin to look for her.

Dennis is stroking my hair. "You've got to let that fear go," he whispers. "Don't defeat yourself before you start."

And I want to believe him. That I can let it go. That I can keep my duty to myself, to my mother, and to Grandma Katherine squarely in mind, without being distracted by what happened to them in marriage. I wish I were as sure as he seems to be.

I test his belief as we walk back to the house. I tell him a little about my idea for the dissertation, about the homestead diaries. "Their writings are almost like poetry, sometimes," I tell him. "Of course, they never would have dreamed of really writing poetry."

"Anyway," Dennis reminds me, "the popular writing style was very flowery and affected just then. It's better they didn't."

I'm feeling easier with Dennis now. I throw my arm around his waist as we walk. "The funny thing is, none of what has happened is really any of your fault," I tell him.

By now, we've made our way through the neighbor's hedge and into my yard. I can discern the metallic gleam of the rusting old swingset frame my parents have never taken down.

Dennis's voice comes to me out of darkness. "You know what you haven't told me," he says. "You haven't said anything about the errand that brought you here in the first place."

"You mean Grandma Katherine," I say. "I suppose that's because there's nothing to be done." And I let the words lie there, flat and ugly. "Unless . . ." I add, thinking aloud.

"Unless what?" Dennis asks.

"What if Grandma Katherine was to come back with me?"

"With us," Dennis corrects.

"Oh, we couldn't cohabit in front of Grandma Katherine. I don't care if she already knows, or suspects our true living situation. She'd be uncomfortable."

"Okay, let's get married," Dennis says.

"Just like that?" I ask.

"My idea is at least worthy of consideration. But go on with what you were thinking. I'm not asking you to consider my proposal now."

"That's it!" And I let out a laugh that sounds rather more like a bark.

He puts his arm around me, squeezes me hard. "You're considering. That's good." He brushes my hair aside and kisses me on the cheek.

"My idea is contingent on a lot of things. For starters, I'd need to borrow some money from somewhere in order to afford a student who could sit with Grandma whenever I couldn't be with her."

"You and I could juggle our schedules around," Dennis suggests. But then he grimaces. "If only the apartment were bigger."

"I see what you mean. It would be hard to get anything done with somebody else around."

"Are you sure now is a good time in your life to try something like this?" Dennis is attempting to keep me grounded in reality.

"I'm sure it's *not*," I reply. "And Grandma Katherine doesn't seem to want to go. But what else can I do? I owe her that much, to try it. Anyway, you're the one who suggested it, indirectly."

"I did?"

"On the phone," I remind him, "you said there had to be other solutions. Well, Mom and Dad have their minds made up about what they're doing and that it's justified and all. I just don't happen to agree. And this is the only solution I can think of that would put me in control."

"I think we need to sleep on it," Dennis says.

So we go inside. I halfway expect Daniel to drop in after his game or his dinner or his whatever. Dennis and I stay up late watching back-to-back "M*A*S*H" reruns just in case Daniel comes through the door. He doesn't. We're both so tired we can barely make it up the stairs and into our separate beds—although it seems an unkindness not to be able to sleep together again after our separation.

IN THE MORNING, Dennis rouses me with a tap on my door. "You up?" he asks quietly.

"Be right down," I answer.

Not long afterward, we're walking hand-in-hand across the lawn. All of the previous night's talk is behind us.

We chop apples for the cider most of the morning, and Daniel shows up in time to turn the crank for the pressing. I'm relieved Susan doesn't come and it's just us. The dog trots around inspecting the whole enterprise, then goes to pant under the tree, her energy and curiosity spent. The temperature has climbed into the sixties. The first cider Mom draws off tastes refreshing, surprisingly cool.

Dad rinses out all the plastic milk jugs with the garden hose.

Mom smiles at Dennis and says, "This is the sort of thing we'd never do alone anymore. It's on account of you."

"Here's to Dennis!" Dad proclaims, raising his cup.

"Hey, everybody—I've got to bow out, now," Daniel breaks in, and upends his cup to drain it. "Laura, you ought to come along. You too, old man." And Daniel claps Dennis on the shoulder. "Some old friends of Laura's and mine are going to be there today."

"We're going over to Grandma's. But tell them I said hello. Or—what is the old-fashioned phrase?—remember me to them. I like that better."

Daniel smiles almost gently at me. "I forget, the one you'd really care to see wouldn't be there. Poor old Victor." He shakes his head. Then he looks up at me. "Did Dennis ever hear tell of Victor?"

He hasn't. Dennis looks at me as though intrigued by this mention of my past life.

"We used to hang out together," I say off-handedly. That's all there was to it. We weren't in love.

Dennis searches my face for more information. He isn't satisfied.

"He was a nice, gentle fellow. We played in the orchestra together. Went to statewide competitions and all that. But he was killed in Vietnam."

Dennis pushes me for nothing more. "Poor guy," he says.

"Well, I'm outta here. Dennis, good meeting you," Daniel says, and then he is gone.

Dennis and I are left to finish the pressing, taking turns at the crank, drawing off gallon after amber gallon of cider.

THE FLOOR NURSE raps briskly on Grandma Katherine's door. No answer. Then, after another moment, she raps again and pushes it open. Grandma Katherine, who is dozing in the armchair, startles awake. She looks so tiny, sitting with her legs curled up underneath her, her chin resting on her chest. She composes herself, but not quickly. I apologize for disturbing her, coming without notice.

Her hands are trembling on her lap. "Laura, I'm always glad to see you, so long as you don't mind—." She stops, sensing another person's presence.

"This is Dennis," I say. "Dennis, my grandma Katherine."

"Oh, excuse me, excuse me," Grandma Katherine dusts off her pants legs with nervous hands. "I wish you had let me know *he* was coming," she reprimands me. "It's good to meet you. Dennis, well, . . ." she says, readjusting herself in her seat.

"Dennis has come to take me back to Chicago, where I belong," I tell her.

She smiles at me. "Good," she says.

"I think I'm ready to get back to work on my dissertation."

"Something's happened, then."

"Yes. I started thinking, like a drowning person, about what to hold on to."

Dennis is frowning at me. I can tell he disapproves of what I am telling her. His eyebrows puzzle up over the bridge of his nose, his lips curl into a half-hearted sneer—his face is strangely lovely and compelling that way.

"That's how I felt," I insist. "Afterward, when I had decided to go back, I tried to think as rationally as I could about my choices. I'm going to do a project on homesteading women's diaries. Remember that article I did once? I showed you."

The wrinkles around Grandma Katherine's mouth soften. "Oh, yes. Now, there's something I could help you with. If only there was a way for me to do the research. Just to be able to look out for things, even, and keep them clipped."

"I know," I say. We both know she can't.

I remember Grandma Katherine telling me about the Iowa countryside, the way it was back when she was a girl. She told me how, when she looked out her window at night, the prairie rode out in all directions like a dark sea. Later on, when electricity came, houses appeared like ships anchored beyond the glare of the outbuildings. And I vaguely remember visiting once at the home of my great-grandparents when I was a child (I would have been young, they both died before I was ten), looking out from the porch and wondering whether it would be possible to run through the darkness to the safety of the next beacon. I recall being frightened on the farm, lying in a vast bed with musty-smelling sheets. I trembled at night, unable to fall asleep. The visit was a trip back for my mother, and it's just as well she took me that time because we never had another chance. Grandma Katherine's parents had been the grandparents my mother loved best. Now that I look back on it, I realize Grandma Katherine probably loved them too, even though she had rebelled against them by moving so far away.

My great-grandparents had a stake in the land, and in the community. They were dedicated and active members of the Lutheran church. And the farm houses were closer together in Iowa than farther west, but it was still a considerable distance of a half mile or mile to the nearest neighbor. So, loneliness was Grandma's companion in her youth. If there was ever time for her to be lonely. I'm sure, if Grandma Katherine could do the research with me, the voices of the homesteaders would have resonance for her. And suddenly, I see the tack I'm going to have to take if I'm ever going to convince her to come back to the Midwest with us.

Grandma Katherine says, "I wish I were just starting out again. I wish I had all your time."

11

As WE DRIVE WEST, my reference point is the blue line of hills to the south, the last vestige of the Alleghenies. The line dwindles gradually and will soon disappear. The vineyards, too, will soon vanish as the land is ironed out and we we cross the broad flood plain.

When I was a girl, I helped with the grape harvest, going out into the chill October mornings in a raggy sweater and sneakers wet with dew. I recall the heavy stickiness of the fruit and how the yellow jackets would torment me as I bent my head under the low-hanging vines and did my work. The grapes, once skinned, would fill a vat. I would stick my forearms in, with my eyes squeezed shut—cat's eyeballs.

I ask Grandma Katherine, who is stretched across the back seat but not dozing yet, whether the grapes have been harvested. She barely lifts her head and says mildly, "They're gone."

"The vines all look bare to me," Dennis says.

And I heave a sigh and press down harder on the accelerator. I've made my last break with that place. Again.

Across the Indiana border, we take a rest stop. I turn and look over my shoulder, half-expecting Grandma Katherine to be asleep. She is sitting bolt upright, with a knowing expression on her face. I'm relieved I don't have to disturb her.

"I'm not going inside," she announces.

Well, fine. Dennis can run to the men's room while I'm filling the car. I can wait until he comes back. Grandma Katherine waits until the my back is turned— when I'm at the booth paying for gas—to get out of the car. And when I look back, she is gone. I freeze a moment in panic. Dennis is headed back across the pavement. I run toward him, waving my arms.

"She's gone. I don't know how she disappeared so quickly. I was never more than fifteen feet from the car." I glance around anxiously as semi-trailers rumble by.

Dennis and I have covered the parking lot and are about to go in to search the bathrooms and the restaurant, when I suddenly remember: She said she wouldn't go in there. "Dennis, let's try the picnic ground," I say.

There we find her, holding on to one of the tables, listing slightly to one side.

"Grandma Katherine!" I cry. "I thought you were going to wait inside the car."

She turns in the direction of my voice. Did she realize she was facing out toward a view of a cornfield beyond the chain link fence? "That's not what I said," she says firmly.

"Okay, we misunderstood you. But I was worried. You could have been hit by a truck."

"I didn't hear any trucks," Grandma Katherine says.

"You were lucky, then," Dennis says, taking her by the arm.

"Not yet." She pushes him away. "The breeze is so refreshing."

"It's exhaust," I whisper to Dennis.

We stand with Grandma Katherine for a few moments in silence before she turns to lead us back to the car.

"You're sure there's nothing you need while we're here—a drink, a trip to the bathroom?" I ask her.

She shakes her head.

"I don't know if it's a good idea to leave without taking her into the bathroom, at least," I whisper to Dennis.

My parents had given me that warning when I told them of my plans to bring Grandma Katherine to Chicago with me. Of course, I lied and said I only planned a brief sojourn. I made no mention of my hopes that my grandma would choose to live with me and never again return to The Evergreens.

"What can we do?" Dennis whispers back. "She says she doesn't want to."

Soon after we pull back onto the interstate, Grandma Katherine sleeps. Dennis pulls out a journal and reads. After miles of gently undulating cornfields, I feel somnolent myself. The sky is beginning to take on an opaque cast as the light wanes, though there are still two hours left until the sunset. These late fall afternoons when the light is withheld depress me so, I think back to my Munch print, the one I couldn't bear to hang on my apartment wall after I met Dennis. And I consider Grandma Katherine, how the light is withheld from her. Bleak northwest Indiana, with its unnerving roadside crosses, the hellish refinery vats, stretches ahead of me. I tense up, but the landscape fails to affect me in precisely the same way it once did. I know I can pass through unscathed. I can look at the howl-faced man on the bridge without becoming one with him, without being pulled in by his strange energy.

Before long, we're passing through industrial South Chicago. Dennis puts his reading down, and we stare together out the window past the spectacle of the skyline rising on the horizon. Some subtle change of attitude alerts Grandma Katherine. She sits up and leans forward, grasping at Dennis's arm. I realize, with a shock of recognition, that she *belongs* to us, and that Dennis has found acceptance with her.

"Are we in the city yet?" Grandma Katherine asks.

Dennis turns to face her. "For the last five minutes or so," he answers. "How long is it since you've been back?"

"At least . . ." She heaves a sigh. "I don't know, a long time."

"Seven or eight years, I think. Remember, you came along on a Midwestern trip when I was still in high school and Mom and Dad were helping me decide on a college?"

But Grandma Katherine isn't listening. "Do you know the Edgewater Beach Hotel?" she asks Dennis, in a confidential tone of voice.

"I think so. Is it pink?"

"Yes, that's the one. It was always a landmark of sorts."

"It's on the north side, right? Over by the lakeshore?"

"Right. Charles and I used to go to dances there. So it's still standing, is it?"

"I don't think it has dancing anymore," he says. "But it's there."

"Was this after you were married, Grandma?"

"We went once a month while we were courting. After we were married, maybe a couple of times a year, with friends."

"What was it like?" I ask.

"Swank," she says, and flashes us a grin. "Terribly sophisticated. And how we dressed! I can remember squandering my salary on something new, even though I knew Charles wouldn't have approved. Other gals sewed up masterpieces in satin, with tucks and bows and fabric roses, but I didn't like to sew."

And her voice drifts into a wistful sigh as we negotiate the grid of one-way streets near my apartment.

AFTER A RESTLESS NIGHT spent on my fold-out sofa, I become alert to sounds of movement—floorboards creaking, a door easing open or shut—perhaps from the apartment above. I take notice of the still-gray sky—the sun has yet to rise—and am about to dismiss the sounds when I hear a crash followed by a terrified yowl.

Grandma Katherine! I remember, and bump into the end table in my rush to get to her in time.

I find her leaning against the sink. The tap is turned on high; pieces of broken glass swirl in the sink. I resist my urge to ask what happened, and say, "It's okay, it's okay."

I repeat these words over and over again like a mantra, but she shakes with panic. I'm not sure she knows where she is.

I castigate myself for not thinking ahead to how disoriented she'd be waking up in a strange place. I keep talking to her in a soft voice as I clean up the bathroom and help her settle into my one comfortable chair. I remember what she used to like for breakfast, and do my best to fix it: orange juice, thin-sliced toast, a soft-boiled egg.

White chunks of egg swim around in their yolk on my plate. I haven't had this breakfast in years. It tastes wonderful.

I swipe my plate with my toast, mopping up every stray drop of yolk, and then devour the toast.

"Do you live near the lake?" Grandma Katherine asks, wiping the corner of her mouth with a tissue I set out in lieu of a napkin.

"It's a block and a half away," I say, clearing our plates. "There's a little park."

A smile crosses Grandma Katherine's face. "I think I would like to hear the lake again."

"We'll stop there," I say, "on our way back from class. Let's get ready."

I help Grandma Katherine sort through her suitcase. There isn't a lot of extra storage space in my apartment, so I figure she'll just have to keep things folded inside the suitcase's sturdy hull. Whenever she wants something, she'll have to unzip the plaid fabric top.

Getting Grandma Katherine ready takes so much time, I have to forego my shower. I yank on yesterday's jeans. I can't find the right notebook for my morning class, but I shrug into my coat anyway. "Let's go!" I yell.

I rush with Grandma Katherine down the sidewalks, pulling her along perhaps more forcefully than I should, but we still arrive late. The sleepy faces which turn to watch us enter pinch into puzzled expressions, except Dennis's face, which opens with a look of relief.

Professor Baird turns from the chalkboard to remark on my arrival. "She's back!" He watches me help my grandma into a seat and says, "And you've even brought a friend."

I smile and bow my head as I sit beside her, but after a moment, I realize I should have introduced Grandma Katherine while I had the opportunity.

As I watch Baird diagram Williams' "The Yachts," a poem I have never liked or understood well, I slouch in my chair. Dennis leans forward with appetite—"The Yachts" is one of his favorite poems. And it is beautiful to the ear, at the same time being terrible to comprehend. I know that. But I have no patience in seeking out the roots of the poem's metaphor. I tap my pencil on my notebook.

"Last week, we did 'Of Asphodel,'" Dennis whispers to me.

I think longingly back to those familiar broken lines, how they would have inspired me today. During the "Yachts" discussion, I scribble verbatim notes, hoping to later reconstruct whatever it is I'm now unwilling to harvest from the poem.

I hear the sound of water spilling. Then I spot the source: liquid is running down Grandma Katherine's chair and pooling on the floor. I assumed she had been to the bathroom before we left the apartment, but I hadn't checked with her to be sure. I brace myself for Grandma Katherine to cry out, but she remains silent. I fish in my purse for tissues, then blot the edge of her chair. At least the chair is molded plastic and the floor is tile. I drop two tissues to absorb the spill, then sit up as if I'm paying especially acute attention. Only fifteen minutes left to go. I glance around, but no one else seems to have noticed.

I let everyone else filter out ahead of us, even Dennis, who hurries through the crowd and says, "I'll call you this afternoon."

Professor Baird touches his hand to my shoulder, and I jump.

"Everything all right, Laura?" he asks.

I hold my own breath, hoping he doesn't register the stench of urine that clings to Grandma Katherine and me.

I begin to chatter nervously: "Dennis probably let you know—I had a family emergency two weeks ago and had to go out of town. Actually, I'd like you to meet my grandmother, Katherine Schrier. She's got a Master's in English from the University of Buffalo. She'll be visiting me until the end of the term. I hope you won't mind if I bring her to class."

"It'll be fine," he says. "Unofficially, of course." He pats me once on the back. "Drop by sometime during my office hours this week, all right? I think we've got a few issues to discuss if I'm to advise you."

I know that if Grandma Katherine weren't beside me, he'd put his arm around my shoulders and ask to walk with me, or request that I join him for a cup of coffee. But this time, I wave him out of the room, so that I can properly clean up. Then Grandma Katherine and I walk home along the lakefront, the way I had promised. The weather has changed while we were inside. The breeze is stiffer, and it blows at an angle to the lake. Each wave, as it breaks, appears to bend backwards before ponderously crashing against the jetty, shattering on the rocks.

"It's rough, isn't it?" Grandma Katherine lifts her face toward the lake.

I nod. The wind is raw; it brings tears to my eyes. The whitecaps are flecks of interference on a field of gray, like a movie screen before the film spools through the projector. I'm crying, not just stinging tears from the cold, but really crying. I wipe my face with my knuckles.

"Come on, let's go," I say in my husky voice. I worry that the bitter wind will chill Grandma Katherine, blowing through her wet things. We hurry past the sights of the park—the snowsuit-bound toddlers in their strollers, and chattering, oblivious mothers; the occasional bikers, hunched low against the wind; the lone woman out feeding birds. I don't have the time to describe these things to her.

"I'm awfully tired," Grandma Katherine says, pulling against me to stop our progress.

I wait for a moment, then suggest, "We'd better be getting back. Come on, you can lean on my arm."

And she does. Her weight is almost hard to bear. Several times, her body threatens to collapse on me. It's as if she has lost the will to place one foot in front of the other. Somehow we arrive at my apartment in time for lunch.

After canned soup and cold sandwiches, Grandma Katherine dozes in the armchair. Although I changed her clothes, I didn't manage to get her to the bathroom again, and my afternoon seminar starts in half an hour. Down at the mailboxes, I run into Lila, from upstairs. She asks about Grandma. I tell her about the day's mishaps. Lila, a mother of young children, shakes her head, and her long hair ripples. She's a lithe, beautiful young woman. It's not difficult to guess that she's a dancer, but surprising to imagine her with babies.

She says, "It's like having children. All of a sudden, everything you do depends on someone else."

Lila is right. I close the door behind me and make an effort to read something that will be "of use" in lieu of going to the seminar. I realize that I need to go to the library. Every book I'm burning to read is one more book I don't have on my overstuffed bookshelves. If only I could get Grandma Katherine in the right state of mind to accompany me. She might enjoy the errand. And I could check out some books on tape for her. The university has some marvelous recordings—things Grandma

Katherine has been deprived of by the budgetary con-
straints on the local library back in Felicity.

I anxiously check my watch. The seminar is just start-
ing. I pick up the Winnick text on Robert Frost, although
I hate to read it. But then I hear footsteps in the hall. It's
Dennis! He used his key instead of buzzing up for me.

What a relief it is to be able to recount the events of the
day with him, to sit with him while Grandma Katherine
naps. "I'm glad you're here," I say. "But a little surprised."

"Didn't I tell you I would help out? And don't you have
that seminar on translation just now? So I'll stay, you go.
Later on tonight, we'll sit down and work out a schedule."

I gently close the door, full of gratitude. I'm not sure I
would have done the same for him. I am parsimonious
when it comes to giving of myself and my time.

The day has been difficult for me. Sometimes I wish
that I were fluent in French so I could translate some of
those poets—Paul Claudel, for instance. But today, I lose
myself in the Rilke's elegies, unraveling the German syn-
tax and groping for a sense of his pattern and rhythm. On
the tenth elegy, I come to the part where the man, just
having died, cannot see. The German verb is *erfaßt*.
Except it's more subtle than that, and I cannot be literal.
His is a very non-literal journey. Is Grandma Katherine,
too, journeying toward new vision?

I've always known that there are other planes of
awareness, and that I can be informed by them, and yet
their presence has been newly brought to my attention.

Sailing out from the seminar on my exhilaration, I
impose on Dennis's generosity a few minutes longer, picking up a few books and some tapes for Grandma

Katherine at the library. Just a few, then I can bring her back with me. I'll spend long hours in the library, sifting through boxes of letters and mementos in the Special Collection. While the mellow amber light of midwinter afternoon slants in through the windows, I'll search for a common thread, a truth—now that I know what I am looking for.

I race up the stairs to my apartment, breathing hard. Dennis and Grandma Katherine are engaged in a game of gin rummy. His admiring eyes fasten on me. "Something's done you good," he says. "Was it the walk, or class?"

"Both. It's good to think in abstractions. It's been a while," I say.

"While you've been gone, Katherine here has taken me to the cleaners."

Grandma Katherine puts her hand up to her mouth and chuckles. Dennis has managed to charm her.

He stands up and stretches out his long limbs. Suddenly, I desire him and picture him all lovely, the way he gets when he's full of ardor, when his mouth softens and his eyes intensify.

"Mind my staying for dinner?" Dennis says. "I'll even cook the meal."

I don't want Dennis to go after supper. I wish to curl up and purr under his touch like a cat. Grandma Katherine is tucked in bed. I'm going to have to adjust to her pattern of tiring early in evening, waking early in morning. There are a lot of practical reasons why Dennis shouldn't stay, but he stays anyway. I set an early alarm.

"Grandma Katherine can't suspect this," I whisper to him. "She wouldn't understand."

"I think you underestimate her," Dennis says.

We don't speak further of Grandma Katherine this evening.

I AM AWAKENED, AGAIN, more than an hour after poor Dennis stole off, unshowered and unshaven, and I reentered a barely lapsed sleep. I groan and roll from my bed. I hear the agitated slamming of dresser drawers in the next room. I rush in naked. Grandma Katherine is jerking another drawer out of the bureau, and she doesn't turn towards me. She sifts through the drawer's contents, then slams it shut again. Her strength surprises me.

"Those aren't my things!" she hollers.

My room is in a shambles. Another drawer is overturned on the floor. I have always been an impetuous person, the last person on earth to be patient, but I wrap myself in a robe and sit down on the edge of the bed with her, to calm her down. I try to explain. "Your things are in the suitcase, Grandma; those are mine in the drawer."

And we manage to get dressed and eat, somehow.

I NEED TO REASSURE MYSELF DAILY that Grandma Katherine and I are making progress, falling into some sort of a pattern. I manage to attend most of my classes. On my project, I'm making about half the amount of solid progress I think I should. Professor Baird is an obstacle overcome, though he admitted, leaning back beside me on his office sofa, that he might have to give an extra push to get my project past committee. In return, I will put up with his chummy pats on the back and his arm draped across my shoulder, and listen without comment to his sometimes offensive monologues.

I savor my occasional afternoons at the library—perhaps more so now that getting to the library is so difficult. It occurs to me, as I sift through other women's letters and papers, their diary entries, that now I could write a journal that would begin to sound like the life of a woman. I find myself thinking back to what my neighbor Lila said: *Everything you do depends on someone else.* It sounded awful to me when she first said it. I am beginning to see that, in another sense, the people around me help to define me.

As Grandma Katherine and I enter our third week together, there continue to be the usual mishaps. And I wish I didn't keep her plugged into the audiotape player so much, even though it makes my work at the library possible. During these weeks, as Dennis and I remain faithful to our pact of caring for Grandma Katherine, we resume our own faithfulness to each other. And beneath the surface of his silence, I can sense that he is waiting for some answer, some commitment, from me.

12

EARLY IN DECEMBER, the weather turns unexpectedly mild, making possible an excursion across the border into Iowa to further my research on one of my diarists.

Dennis and I have put a picnic together for the car. I've packed Grandma Katherine a selection of audiotapes and a selection of clothes—sweaters of varying thickness and extra socks, slacks and panties, just in case. She seems excited at the prospect of being in farm country again, so close to where she grew up. She doesn't have anyone left back there. The only close relative who still lives in the state is one of her sisters, but she lives far west, nearer Sioux City.

The first thing Grandma remembers about Iowa when we step from the car is the wind. It's a freshening wind, blowing in from the cornfields. Clouds scuttle low across the vast sky. What must it have been like to live beneath a sky like that and smell that sweet wind?

"It's almost a spring wind," Grandma Katherine remarks. Her face is open, receptive. "Like April. This is the kind of wind that used to bring the birds in. They'd stop at the lake. I remember how their screams and the beating of their wings filled the air."

We're standing on the sidewalk of Main Street beside the car I've angle-parked in front of the café. The town, though a county seat, seems quiet. Some of the buildings are false-fronted, the wood panels on the sides are weather-beaten and stripped of paint. At the end of Main Street, the vista opens up into farmland again. An older man sweeps the sidewalk in front of his shop.

"They drained those lakes years ago. The birds don't come in such numbers anymore," he says to Grandma Katherine. "You come from around here?"

"Betelmans," she answers. "But I moved away to Chicago."

"Name's Hermann Eckhert," he says, extending his hand.

Grandma Katherine doesn't take his hand. She does greet him warmly with a smile. "I'm Katherine Schrier. Used to be Arner."

He looks from his hand up into her eyes. His realization of her blindness registers on his face. "The name's familiar. It's been a good forty years since we've had any lakes hereabouts. I guess it tells you how old I am if I say I remember canoeing on them with my dad."

"Why'd they drain them?" I ask.

"They were swamps, wetlands. My guess is, because of all the mosquitoes," Dennis says.

"Ja, you're right," the shopkeeper says with a nod. "People thought they carried disease. A health risk. You know, at the far end of town, there's a park they put out on one of the old lake beds. You should go out and visit if you have the time."

Dennis takes Grandma Katherine's arm. They disappear into the café to have coffee while I look up some records at the courthouse.

I spend most of my time at the Historical Society, emerging half an hour later with no change left, a sheaf of xeroxed papers, and a copy of the town history I purchased for two dollars and fifty cents.

I'm out of breath and apologetic when I join Grandma and Dennis at the café. "Let's do the library tomorrow. I'd just as soon go out to the park now and get some fresh air. Grandma, would it be too much for you to walk down to the park? I'd like to have a look at the town."

But by the time we reach the park—and stop to read the sign put up by the local Chamber of Commerce, listing past presidents back to the early 1950s—Grandma is ready for a rest. Once ensconced upon a bench, she waves us away, saying. "Take a few minutes for yourselves," she says. "I'll be fine."

I do believe she will be, so Dennis and I go off together. No one could easily go out of sight in these surroundings, though there is more roll and dip to the prairie than I had imagined. As we move farther off, Grandma Katherine's figure doesn't disappear; it only recedes, grows smaller.

I'm glad to be alone with Dennis. I rest my head in the hollow of his neck. Grandma Katherine has become more inscrutable recently. She is holding herself back from us, as if to let us see how we'll do without her. The closeness I had hoped to build with this visit eludes me. She seems to take less of an interest in things which were once her passions.

"*Hello*," Dennis says. "What are you thinking about?"

"I'm sorry," I say. "I'm preoccupied with something else. And here it is one of the few times we've been alone lately."

"That it is." Dennis chuckles. "We're getting a taste of what it will be like someday when we have babies."

"You're making a lot of assumptions about the future," I remind him. We kiss, but my mood remains pensive. "It isn't working, is it?"

"I wouldn't say that, exactly." Dennis touches my hair. "I've been able to observe a beautiful part of you I hadn't seen before. I think the affection you have for your grandmother is lovely."

"The term's coming to an end," I say. "I'm not sure I'm going to be able to return with Grandma Katherine for winter quarter, although I'd like to. I'm not even sure it would be the best thing for her, if I could."

Dennis brushes his fingertips across my cheek. "It hasn't been easy to care for her," he says. "I don't know anyone who'd blame you if you thought it was too much."

"It's not that. I'm surprised I haven't felt more over-whelmed. There was the initial shock of having someone so dependent on me, but I got over that. I've almost start-ed to like it." I pause a moment, take in that realization.

"No," I say. "What worries me is that I'm just not sure she's been happy in Chicago."

"You've done some things with her she's really enjoyed."

"She's had her moments. But I don't think she feels secure here, somehow. I've got to keep this in perspective, remember that I want her with me for her sake, not mine."

The wind has turned insistent. I shiver. Dennis is star-ing intently at me with his blue-black eyes.

When we look away from each other, Grandma Katherine still rests on the bench. She is sitting with her head tilted slightly back, as if to catch the sun on her face. I see her clearly from this distance, but I sense she is smiling. I turn back to Dennis. An uncannily warm wind riffles through my hair. Smudgy clouds are crowding in to fill the sky.

"Do you think it's going to rain?" I say.

"Looks like they've been parched here. It would do the land good." Dennis pulls me back into an embrace. "Laura, let's get married," he says. "Whatever you decide about Katherine."

"Yes," I say.

"I don't believe it!" Dennis shouts, lifting me off the ground and swinging me around.

There is a subdued roar of thunder, and the first few heavy drops of rain begin to fall. As we run back to Grandma Katherine, the drops come faster.

In the car, Grandma Katherine is particularly lucid. With the thunder rumbling overhead and the rain streaming down, she says that she can sense a ceiling above. A picture of clouds moving overhead is coming back in her mind. The vision is so delicious to her that she savors it and takes no notice of Dennis and me singing along with the radio in the front seat.

"I REMEMBER AUNT BERTI'S HOUSE," Grandma Katherine says. "The gardens especially. You know, I can still see them. There was a rose arbor, and a pond with lilies and goldfish. Uncle Otto had built Berti a summer house, and we used to sit under there and play cards."

"Do you remember where it was?" Dennis asks.

"On the corner of Grove Avenue and Second Street," Grandma replies.

Dennis is behind the wheel, driving down an arrow-straight stretch of highway which will lead us straight into Betelmans.

"What about the farm?" I ask.

"It's on the old post road on the way up to Mason City."

"Whatever happened to it?"

"Oh, it was given to my brother, Willy, after my father died. My mother moved in with Aunt Berti for her last couple of years. But when Willy died, it was sold off."

"Wasn't Aunt Berti your father's sister?"

"Yes, and she and Mother were very different—Berti was more sophisticated, and Mother was more generous, kinder. But, in the end, they became pretty dependent upon each other."

Dennis drives down Grove Street, and I spot the house, which is white with an expansive lawn, but it is impossible to see whether the gardens still exist. There appear to be beds, but they are barren; even the weeds have gone dormant. It's the time of year—after the leaves have been swept up and yards raked, when everything has ceased growing—when the starkness of the landscape can come as a relief.

The rain has stopped. We park the car and stand at the edge of the sidewalk, staring at what must be, for us, an imaginary garden. It's an eerie feeling. I've been here before, in another lifetime, being hugged and fussed over by women I know only as faded faces in a photograph album. I remember being taken over to see the fish swimming in the pond, my older cousin holding me by the hand.

I glance over at Grandma Katherine. She doesn't have to resolve the incongruity of a new image. Then, I see something she described from memory. "Look, the arbor's still there," I say.

Grandma Katherine says: "Ah, I remember that spot. That's where Charles proposed to me. We had just come

in from strolling alone in the far section of the lawn. In
the arbor, we were almost hidden. I remember looking
out from there—some kind of big event was going on, the
tables were laid out under the trees and there were lovely tall layered cakes with strawberries and whipped
cream. All the relatives were there. Great-aunt Karen was
leaning over the table, talking loudly in German and
wagging her finger. I knew that when Charles and I
emerged from the arbor, we'd be stepping into our new
life. In their eyes, I'd never be the same.

"But then, I had to take on a whole new identity," she
says. "Not like it will be for you."

"Grandma," I say, "Dennis and I are getting married.
We just decided."

"Oh!" Grandma claps her hands together. "I knew it!
I'm glad to see the day. When we get home," she says,
"remind me. I have something I'd like to give to you. It's
a photograph my cousin's husband took of us that afternoon, in front of the arbor. I think it shows some of the
gardens, as well."

We stroll down Grove Street, because Grandma says it's
only a two-block walk to the Lutheran church her father
and brothers helped to build. She remembers working to
prepare some of the big communal meals for men who
worked on the "new" church. The original Grove
Lutheran Church burned down after being struck by
lightning.

"I bet I'm one of the few people around who would
remember that fire, too," Grandma Katherine says. "It
turned the sky pink. We could even see it from the farm.
Two other buildings were lost as well. And if it hadn't
been for the downpour that came along, we might have
lost more.

"I had dreams about that fire for years," she says. "Even after I moved away."

As we come up the walk of the new church, which is nearly seventy years old, I strain to imagine the burnt-out skeleton of the church that had been. Two elderly women emerge from a side door, each bent over with a burden. But, almost immediately, one of them puts down her bag and rushes toward us. She throws up her arms. "Katherine Arner! I'm right, aren't I? I'm Anna, Anna Reiss. I used to live next door to your aunt. You were always hiding in those bushes so we could never find you."

A smile comes over Grandma's face. "I remember. You had the beautiful long brown braids. Always with ribbons. And didn't we used to play with a dollhouse you had up in the attic?"

"Yes, yes, that's right."

"I'm sorry I didn't recognize you. I've lost my sight, you know."

The old woman, Anna, shakes her head. "I'm sorry to hear it."

By now, Anna's companion has joined us. She is a stout woman, not wispy like the other two, and wears a bright floral scarf on her head. It's hard to imagine these three as children, as playmates, but if I look carefully enough, I can see in their animated faces a glimpse of how they might once have looked.

The women lead Grandma Katherine inside to meet the young new pastor. Dennis and I follow behind, pausing to read the dedication in the hall. Soon, Grandma Katherine and her friends rejoin us, and the pastor guides us on a short tour which ends outside the sanctuary.

"You weren't here for the funeral?" the pastor asks Grandma.

"No," Grandma Katherine frowns. "Whose funeral was it?"

"Thomas Hesse's."

"Thomas Hesse!" she cries out. No one notices Grandma Katherine's gasp but me.

"You would have known some people at the funeral," Anna says. "Lucky we stayed to break down the bouquets. If only you had come along half an hour earlier, so many of our friends were here!"

"Whatever happened to him?" Grandma Katherine asks quietly.

"He survived his wife by thirty years," Hilde, the stout lady, answers. "It wasn't good for him, living all those years alone out on the farm."

Anna nods—it must be the general consensus of the town that Thomas Hesse's isolation changed him. "But, before that, he was a good man," Anna says.

Grandma Katherine says nothing to disclose her feelings for Thomas. She heaves a sigh, and from then on, her face is clouded over.

Anna and Hilde exchange a look, as if they're considering what to say. "A few people have gone over to his son's house. You could help us, if you wanted, with the leftovers from the buffet."

The two women know something, too, and this invitation is as close as they'll come to acknowledging it.

Even though subdued, Grandma Katherine appears torn between her curiosity and the impropriety of joining fellow mourners at the home of Thomas Hesse's son. The news of this man's passing has made her pensive, turned her inward.

"It's so different, so different from what I expected," Grandma Katherine mutters as we return to the car. "But why should it be otherwise? They lived a whole life, and I was inconsequential to it.

"I made a choice," she declares. And then, in a softer voice she says, "Thomas proposed to me once, just before I was about to go away to college. He was a lovely boy— strapping, smart, and proud. I left anyway, and he wasn't the type to ask again."

She shakes her head. "I can't believe Anna ended up marrying that awful Gunter Kraft, after all. She had too much spunk to be put down by a man. But he was her second husband. The first time around, she married too young. Maybe the second time, her parents insisted upon having a say."

It's almost too much, too overwhelming for Grandma to visit the farm now, but we drive there anyway. We may never have another opportunity to see it together. Grandma Katherine had told us before how the farm had gone to her brother Willy. His other siblings considered him to be somewhat of an idiot, and I add that detail to the story Dennis knows while Grandma catnaps in the backseat. I speculate that the farm had to be sold because Uncle Willy had died unmarried and childless. The other siblings were scattered all around the country and had no interest in farming.

Neither Dennis nor I wants to describe the abandoned farm house and wind-blown outbuildings to Grandma Katherine. She stands a few feet apart from us in the courtyard between the house and the barns, where trucks used to pull in and load years ago. The gravel is over-grown with weeds.

"Is anybody home?" Grandma asks.

We have to tell her, no, there isn't. We're free to push open the door, to walk through the dingy rooms which reveal no memories to me but must to Grandma Katherine, because she lingers in them.

I step back outside. The nearby fields had all been cultivated this past season.

"They're probably all part of some big corporate spread now," Dennis says, coming out of the house to stand beside me.

I try to push away the flicker of annoyance at hearing him explain something that I already know.

The farmhouse yard is still bordered by a weathered picket fence that sags in the sections. An inoperable wooden swing rests on a porch collapsing beneath the weight of unpruned wisteria vines. In the yard stand bare shade trees, which will leaf out again in spring above the overgrown tufts of prairie grasses.

"Goodbye," I whisper to the yard, as I climb back into the car. And I know that I'm giving the yard, with the endless fields that spread beyond, a place in my memory.

TWO WEEKS LATER, Dennis, Grandma, and I are in Felicity for Christmas break. We are seated at the dining room table with all of the family—aunts, uncles, and cousins included. Outside the window, snow swirls against a dark field. The dinner my mother planned to celebrate my engagement is cut short by the news of snow squalls. Uncle Kurt has already excused himself from the table twice to check outside on road conditions. Now Daniel flicks on the radio, and we hear that the interstate is closed. I wonder how Dennis and I will manage to make the drive back to see his family for Christmas. One by one the family drifts from the table. Only Grandma Katherine remains seated. I want to go to her, but it's hard for me to make my way against the tide of relatives clamoring to bid me goodbye. Her face has gone slack, and I sense she is overweary. This is not her family; they all belong to my dad. I'm also concerned that she may be feeling ill, that the lingering cold she caught during our trip to Iowa may have taken a turn for the worse.

Uncle Kurt pats me on the cheek with his leather-gloved hands. "Sorry, honey, we would have liked to stay."

And, in small groups, the relatives begin to take their leave. Aunt Marianne flutters by in her gray coat and frosted hair. Susan hugs me goodbye, and Dan forgets himself for a minute and tries to shake my hand. Aunt Bett looms before me, one corner of her lip turned down in a funny smile. She embraces me, then holds me at arm's length and studies me. Her chin is quivering, and she looks forlorn, despite her best efforts to beam. Uncle Mike, Bett's husband, smiles to me from the background—where he lives in Bett's shadow. He has spent most of the evening absent from the table, following after his grandson Jason, an active toddler.

Grandma Katherine joins me at the threshold, and Dad helps her put on her coat. She is riding with Daniel and Susan back to The Evergreens. Her breathing is a little labored.

"I think you should arrange for her to get to a doctor tomorrow," I say softly to Dad. "I think there's a van that'll drop her off for her appointment."

By tomorrow, weather permitting, Dennis and I will be gone. I hug Grandma Katherine briefly, take one last look at her bewildered face, her frazzled halo of white hair.

"Come back inside, you're not even wearing a coat," my mother scolds, having suddenly appeared at my elbow.

I let her draw me back inside, although a part of me still lingers out there, in the snowy darkness, with Grandma.

"Have a cup of coffee," my mother says. "The dishes will wait."

And I do. We sit at the kitchen table, which is strewn with little gifts. Mom serves my coffee in her best china teacups. We kick off our shoes and stretch our feet out under the table.

"Do you have some room left?" Mom asks. "There are just two slices of the chocolate-raspberry roll, and it doesn't keep."

"All right," I say. I am full, but there is really nothing like my mother's chocolate raspberry roll, with its plump fruits and glaze of bittersweet chocolate.

"This is still my favorite dessert," I declare, nibbling at the saturated cake.

"Mmmm. . . ." Mom sips her coffee. "Someday you may be the one hosting these family dinners. I'll have to write the recipe down for you."

From out in the dining room, I can hear the clink of plates as Dennis stacks them. I think of Grandma Katherine, the party of ghosts that celebrated her engagement. But only sixty years ago, they were as real as we are: the long tables covered with white linen sheets, the balmy air, her uncles with their sleeves rolled up, and her aunts spoon-feeding their infants who now have to wear reading glasses and use canes.

Mom shakes her head. "Poor Bett. Having that grandchild in the house is running her ragged.

"I know, everybody says you could see it coming, she's gotten what she deserves. But I don't think anybody deserves that in middle age, grown children still in the house and having to mother little babies all over again," Mom says.

I sip my coffee. "Mom," I say, "do you think Grandma will make it to Dan's wedding?"

Mom's face drops a little, and I feel sorry that I've brought the subject up. But then she says, "I don't see any reason why not, but I'm not going to be able to worry about her. Maybe looking after her can be your charge."

"I wouldn't mind."

"I know." Mom looks me straight in the eye. "Not many granddaughters would have done what you did for your grandmother. Your father and I respect you for it, you know."

She does not say she understands my choice, just that she respects my opinion, but that is more than I expected. "Thanks," I say, pushing myself away from the table. I cross over to the kitchen sink and start the hot water running. Mom joins me at the counter with a cloth.

"Tell me about the farm," she asks. "What was it like?"

I describe the abandoned farmhouse and the sweet April-smelling breeze. I tell her about the town and about Aunt Berti's house, a place that Mom remembers from many childhood excursions. I recount the story of running into Hilde and Anna outside the Grove Lutheran Church after Thomas Hesse's funeral. "They recognized her after fifty years' time, do you believe that?"

Mom hangs on every word, and when I'm done she says, "Maybe you and I could go back and see it together some day."

"Maybe." I'm looking out the window over the kitchen sink. Wind-driven squalls have plastered it with snow. "It's snowing pretty hard right now," I say. "I hope Dan and Grandma are okay."

"And everyone else," Mom says, drawing in a breath, thinking perhaps of that one accident that almost changed our lives.

We're silent for the moment. Everything is. Nothing is so silent as an evening when a thick snow is falling.

13

GRANDMA KATHERINE DIDN'T ATTEND Daniel's wedding, or mine. Nor was she ever well enough to return with me to my apartment in Chicago, although I had made up my mind to oppose the family, if it proved necessary, and take her home with me again. Our visit to Betelmans had convinced me that she no longer belonged to any one place—she had let go of places and belonged where her heart and soul belonged. And I may have been wrong, but I became convinced that her heart and soul belonged with me.

I reinvent her deathbed scene over and over again in my mind out of a need to be there, a need I'll never be able to fill. While I was still in Michigan with Dennis and his family, my parents called to keep me posted on Grandma Katherine's deteriorating health. Mom said that she had spent the evening with them and didn't seem at all well. The doctor couldn't find anything specific and said it was probably just a virus. In two days, I would be driving back to Chicago. I asked my mom if I should drive home instead.

On a Sunday afternoon in January, two days before I was scheduled to take my orals, I received a call from Mother. Grandma had pneumonia and was in the hospital. The doctors treated her with intravenous antibiotics.

I tried to think of what Grandma Katherine would want me to do. I took my orals. By Tuesday night, Grandma had lost consciousness. I had lost my chance to see her one last time. We never had a definitive parting.

Two years later, I still regret that we didn't say good-bye.

Dennis and I have teaching jobs at a small liberal arts college not far from Betelmans. One of my students turned out to be the granddaughter of Grandma Katherine's sister Julia, the one who moved out to South Dakota. We have Christina, Grandma Katherine's great-niece and my distant cousin, out for Sunday dinner when school is in session. Great-aunt Julia is unable to travel, so we've never met. I'm hoping to visit her during the summer, when my schedule is more free.

This past Christmas, Christina and Julia sent me a box of family mementos as a present. It didn't contain a diary—although I asked Great-aunt Julia several times in letters whether anyone in the family had kept one—but there were xeroxed clippings from the local newspaper. Julia sent photographs, accounts of an uncle's accidental death, lists of wedding guests, and recitation prizes. She wrapped up the family bible, and recopied her mother's old recipes. Katherine's sister provided me enough of her treasures to give me a sense of lives which had passed, unrecorded.

From time to time, Dennis and I have taken a picnic out to the abandoned farmhouse yard. We even took Mom and Dad there once. And we've driven past Aunt Berti's former garden in August. It exists, but only as a shadow of its former glory, a magnificence I've since seen in old home movies.

Mother and I talk frequently. We both can see our past conflicts with more equanimity than before. Dad's architectural firm has begun to turn around with business from over the border in Canada. Buffalo, too, may survive the loss of the mills and become a financial center. Felicity itself is changing—something I wouldn't, as a youth, have believed possible. There still are the broad farmlands spreading out from town's center, but more and more old sections of woodland are being sold off and subdivided. Daniel and Susan had better buy that house they've been talking about for two years—its price is going up, just like Dan said it would.

I'm finishing a second book for the university press that published my first, an edited collection of writings by farm wives, entitled *Homesteading Women.* The voices of those women call out across the space of generations with such resonance. I feel how clearly they are my ancestors.

I have begun writing a diary myself. And, any week now, I'll go into labor with my first child. I find myself waking at odd hours, pondering particularly vivid dreams in which I'm seeing my long-lost relatives again. When women give birth, I think it's as much for the sake of all those who came before us as for our own sake. And I wonder who I'm about to meet. I'm hoping she's a girl.

FELICITY by Kristen Staby Rembold is the winner of the **1993 Mid-List Press First Novel Series Award**. Other novels published by Mid-List Press include:

NEWS FROM FORT GOD by William L. Sutherland. The **1992 First Novel Series Award** winner is written from one of those remote places those who desire to "get away from it all" call home. There, in Fairbanks, Alaska—over the thunderous beat of a dog sled race and the plaintive whine of a weakened car battery—Jack Oliver, his wife Ellen, and his best friend Hunter create a community with their sometimes bizarre and confused fellow travelers. "An endearing tall tale . . . warm and witty."—*Booklist.*   (0-922811-17-2, $12.00, paper)

THE PSI DELEGATION by Allan Conan. Embroiled in a bitter divorce and custody battle, neurologist Fray MacKenzie wants to withdraw from the larger concerns of his world, but the grisly murder of his friend and mentor Alex Chatov, a trip to Russia with the Psi Delegation, and a love affair with a beautiful and psychic dissident transform Fray into an uncommon hero. "A good solid thriller brimming with authentic detail and unflagging tension."—*Booklist.*   (0-928811-04-0, $15.95, cloth)

SAME BED, DIFFERENT DREAMS by Hugh Gross. The **1990 First Novel Series Award** recipient, Hugh Gross, paints an intimate portrait of Japanese life with broad strokes of cultural alienation, sensual desire, and emotional hunger. The story of Toshio and Nozomi is the story of modern Japan—a society drifting from its traditional moorings toward an uncertain future. "A finely etched and evocative psychological portrait."—*Booklist.*   (0-928811-11-3, $9.95, paper)

THE UPSTART SPRING by James Nora. This first novel explores the dark side of academic medicine and research through the dramatic birth of the heart-transplantation procedure. It is a cautionary tale of a man driven to achieve in a world where ethical boundaries have blurred in the bright light of fame. "An absorbing debut."—*Kirkus Reviews.*
(0-92811-00-8, $16.95, cloth)

Mid-List Press titles are available through bookstores or may be ordered directly from Mid-List Press, 4324-12th Avenue South, Minneapolis, Minnesota 55407-3218, (612) 822-3733. Mail orders should include $2.00 for shipping and handling. Note: Prices are subject to change without notice.